Margaret in Washington

Also by R. L. Rhyse

Margaret of Greenwich - Margaret and Erika

Margaret at War - Margaret in Tokyo

Margaret and Eve - Margaret and Velda

Margaret and Emily - Margaret and Hillary

Margaret in London - Margaret at Barnard

Margaret at Barnard/Part Two: Deliverance

Margaret in Berlin - Margaret in Manhattan

Margaret and Venla – Margaret: Mother of Twins - Margaret in Moscow

Margaret and Randy

R. L. Rhyse

Margaret in Washington
Book Eighteen in the
Margaret of Greenwich® Series

Wyston Books, Inc.

Margaret in Washington

Wyston Books, Inc. – Middletown, New York

www.magaretofgreenwich.com

www.wystonbooks.com

Margaret in Washington: a novel

Book Eighteen in the Margaret of Greenwich® Series

1. Margaret of Greenwich (Fictitious character)

2. Teenage Girls Fiction

Library of Congress Control Number: 2021944799
ISBN 978-1-7376816-0-1
eISBN 978-1-7376816-1-8

Cover Photo by Morsa Images
Licensed from Getty Images

BISAC: YAF022000 (Girls & Women)
YAF011000 (Coming of Age)
YAF029000 (Law & Crime)

A person who tries to cheat their fate is not only a coward but a fool.

–Margaret

Introduction

Though intending my memoirs to be absolutely accurate, I recognize this impossibility for a writer. Montaigne stated that a writer could not reveal the truth because of self-interest and prejudices, and Andre Malraux wrote that a writer's truth is mostly what they hide. But I have tried.

A mother's life is frantic, filled with rapidly changing events from farce to tragedy to comedy, stories for a novelist or humorist. Yet even as these streamed in the classroom and after studying the children one-by-one I couldn't decode their present or predict their future. Who can see ahead about their children as we stop dreary thoughts and fears, theirs and ours, with a hug and a kiss.

I was observing my toddlers' Montessori class, which the school allowed parents to do. Listening closely as the teacher asked each child what they wanted to be when they grew up. "A doctor like my mother," one child said. "A football player," said a boy. All predictable until a carefully dressed girl spoke.

Costly dress is common in affluent Greenwich but even here her appearance stood out. If an adult, her costuming would be appropriate for a ritzy cocktail party or gallery opening. She hesitated to speak until the teacher pressed.

Margaret in Washington

"Caroline, what would you like to be when you grow up?"

While overlooked by the children, her answer stunned all adults in the room.

"I want to be alive," she said, without the hint of a mischievous smile.

Chapter 1

It can be tough to see what is obvious if you don't want to, as no adult in the classroom did. The children understandably since they didn't fully grasp Caroline's words and the adults because they didn't want to. If they did they would have to act with an uninviting task. A mother's tribe is her family and she does not need more trouble from outside.

I dallied too, comforting myself with the thought that Caroline *must have* misspoken. Didn't the care that someone took with her appearance confirm this? Worry for an ill relative *must have* aroused her response. A working mother's life overflows with her own family's responsibilities, I told myself.

My resolve was shattered when I remembered the previous Sunday's church service, intoned by our minister from long-dead authors and the Bible. Goethe's caution that what is hardest to see is before your eyes. Longfellow's words, "That, like voices from afar off, call us to pause and listen..." And, most powerful of all, those of Jeremiah, "I will save you from the hands of the wicked and rescue you from the clutches of the violent."

To which I added the injunction of Samuel Johnson, "The fact of twilight does not mean you cannot tell day from night." I hoped.

Chapter 2

"Alive" *was* an odd word for the child to use. I had never heard any of my young children speak it before. I wasn't even sure they grasped its meaning. Children often use words without fully understanding them, appearing adult-like long before maturity.

Had one of her parents died? I wondered with a shudder, having been vulnerable to this topic since the recent death of Mother Marie. Who, though not my parent, had greatly influenced my life.

Cultures belittle unfamiliar traditions and what is accepted as religious in one is considered a cult in another. Thus historic African religions, which are nature based, are often disparaged as "voodoo" or "witchcraft."

Santeria is as ancient a religion as Christianity and contains a mythology as complicated and sophisticated as that of ancient Greece. It was born in Nigeria, along the banks of the Niger River, and transplanted to the Americas by slaves. There, to hide their religious and magical practices from the Spaniards, their deities were identified with the saints of the Catholic Church thus combining different religious beliefs. Yet despite the influence of the Catholic Church, Santeria is mostly primitive magic with buried Africa roots.

Though concealed, the Spanish settlers soon realized what the slaves were doing. This caused much persecution and the hiding of their religious practices by conducting them in the forest. Even so the religion prospered, becoming widely adopted throughout the Americas and even in the United States where some of its members became famous. One was Desi Arnez, the husband and co-star of Lucille Ball on their long running, widely watched TV series, *I Love Lucy*. When he sang "Babalu, Babalu, Babalu Aye," he was invoking *Babaluaye*, a powerful Santeria God. Mother Marie, an *iyanifa* (Mother of Ifa), a Santeria priestess and my spiritual guide since childhood, had just died.

Chapter 3

Funerals aren't for the very young since they haven't yet gained an awareness of mortality. They *exist* and their family and friends *exist* and that's that. That their personal world could greatly change would be too frightening for them to think.

Still, I considered taking them to Mother Marie's funeral. She had known my older children and my newborn, Marie, had been named for her. Mother Marie held my baby just weeks before and agreed to ascertain which *Orisha* (Santeria God/patron saint) would accompany Marie through her earthly journey, watching over and protecting her as do loving parents. This, before her initiation or knowledge of the religion since every child is considered born as a child of the Orisha, *omo Orisha.*

As a child of the Orisha, they exhibit archetypal qualities of that Orisha regardless of their sex since there is no consideration of sex in the determination of one's Orisha, Would Marie's guardian be *Oshun* who exuded calm and unconditional love and diplomacy but was also capable of being short-tempered. Or *Oya,* a warrior of great strength who guards the cemetery with its souls of the departed as they journey onward.

Like all mothers, I sought to know my children though only with Mother Marie did I seek knowledge of her Orisha protector. With James and Donna and Asya, my other children, I hadn't asked her to perform the divination ceremony to identify their Orisha, the deity to whom they should appeal in times of need and to whom they should perform special rituals.

Mother Marie had agreed, conducting a cowry shell (seashell) divination to communicate with the Gods. These shells have an opening resembling the human mouth. When the rounded back is removed, the shells have two flat surfaces so that when dropped they fall in a head or tail configuration. Sixteen shells are used for a divination ceremony. When thrown, these total two-hundred-fifty-six (sixteen times sixteen), there being proverbs and instructive stories associated with each.

Though being ninety-seven-years old, Mother Marie's death had been unexpected and before my baby's divination ceremony could be conducted.

Chapter 4

I didn't bring my children to Mother Marie's funeral which, by Santeria tradition, is more celebration than mourning, a passing of life from one plane to the next with the ability to influence the living. Here, to a greater degree than with other religions, the spirit world is very much alive.

Though being born into a fourth-generation, church-attending Mormon family, my path to Santeria was logical. As a child I was diagnosed with the Sanfilippo Disease genetic disorder. my body lacking an enzyme that properly breaks down sugars affecting concentration and behavior. Sufferers of it usually died in their teens and the disease was considered incurable. Mother Marie, who had been tutoring my older sister in French, learned of my affliction and prayed to her saint to guide me. That night she dreamed that my cure lay in the ordinary soybean. She told my mother and I began eating soybeans and became well. This treatment is now considered standard and, were Mother Marie a doctor, she might have been awarded a Nobel prize.

During a later ceremony I was married to the Santeria God, Babaluaiye, the healer of dreadful diseases. Since then I've worn a two-inch square gold locket. Centered within it is a circle containing ancient symbols like Egyptian hieroglyphics. Inside, I placed a lock of my hair and a bit of cigar ash since one of Babaluaiye's enjoyments is smoking cigars. Of course our marriage is spiritual since Santeria is as morally conventional as other religions and more so than the New Age ones.

Mother Marie's funeral (wake or celebration) took place at the Greenwich apartment where she lived which is the same condominium that my biological mother lives (I am adopted), The overflowing crowd was subdued, all being soberly dressed with the men in dark suits and the women in long dresses. There were no children.

Tears filled my eyes as the ceremony began. Mother Marie's oldest son, a local hedge fund manager, seated himself beside me.

Chapter 5

Unlike other religions, Santeria funeral services consist of three parts. The first of the rituals occurs on the day of their death, the second occurs nine days after their death, and the third occurs a year later. Each ceremony is complex, a form of appeasement to ensure that the dead person's soul departs correctly and will not remain behind to haunt the living.

The corpse is dressed in the clothing they wore during their initiation into the religion. Several hours before burial, the priests and priestesses chant in Yoruba and dance around the coffin, calling the deceased by their initiation name. Then one by one the saints are called, beginning with powerful *Eleggua* who watches over ceremonies to see that they are done in a proper and timely way.

During the lengthy, melancholy, complicated ritual a year later, the last ties of the deceased to the material world are broken and their spirit is finally set free.

According to Santeria belief, the dead become members of the *egun* (the ancestors). Though no longer existing in the visible world, they remain interested in the affairs of their descendants, watching over the moral and social order of society and obedience to public norms.

Not all of a family's ancestors are considered egun. Those who died young without fulfilling their destiny and those who were evil and cruel may be respected as members of the family but are not revered as honored ancestors.

Even in the Americas the religion's respect for the dead remains strong. Every ceremony and ritual begins with an invocation of the egun and every priest and many devotees have small shrines to their personal egun in their homes. In Santeria, reincarnation is believed to be reborn into their own family lineage and often children are considered to embody the spirit of a grandparent. Thus, the dead are always part of the family, and may be seen to return in the faces and mannerisms of their descendants.

After a period of rest and relaxation in the good heaven (*orun rere*), most are reborn into the lives and families of their children. But those who have been cruel or wicked or have harmed other people are not allowed to reincarnate. Instead, they are sent to the bad heaven (*orun bururu*), never to be restored to the living and discarded as one does broken pottery.

The ceremony for Mother Marie in tony Greenwich, far from the barren plains of Africa where the religion evolved, had Western elements, just as the religion's ancestors had syncretized African teachings with Christianity to maintain its survival. There were prayers and a short talk by a priest after which attendees shared memories of Mother Marie before silently departing, feeling spiritually renewed.

Mother's Marie's son touched my arm as I rose to leave.

"My mother foresaw her death and left this for you. I was forbidden to open it," he said solemnly.

I held the envelope as we faced each other, speaking ancient Yoruba religious phrases.

"*Aye l'oja, orun n'ile.*" ("The world is a marketplace. The spirit world is home.")

"*Ise Olorun tobi,*" I replied. ("God's work is great and mighty.")

Chapter 6

I sat holding the envelope long after the others left. It felt warm despite knowing how illogical this belief was. Finally, I placed it in my handbag, bade farewell to the mourners that I recognized, and left.

Why was Mother Marie's son forbidden to read her final words and where should I read them? I asked myself. Surely not at home where my arrival would be met by a cacophony from my children and husband too. Here, alone in my car in the stillness of the condominium's underground garage, seemed perfect.

The manila envelope was sealed with mucilage and its metal clasp though not for security. Her commandment alone would have kept anyone but me from opening it. As a Santeria priestess, Mother Marie was considered to hold powers even after death. None would flout her wishes. Nor did I doubt that her final advice to me, though being indirect as always, would be startling. I unfolded the pages and read.

"My child,

"Foreseeing that I was soon to return to our home in the spirit world, as my final act I conducted the divination of sixteen cowrie shells through which the forces of heaven (*orun*) and earth (*aye*) may be unfolded. Performing yours because of the unusual way that you entered our faith and discovered your spiritual husband, Babaluaiye."

That what followed was a story didn't surprise me since this is the way of Yoruba divination. Not commanding but through sacred stories (*patakís*) from which critical advice is to be gained. I lay down the sheets and gazed at the blank concrete wall for some minutes before returning to the page.

Chapter 7

"There is no way to feel closer to the Gods than through their stories," Mother Marie once told me. Thus I studied her words, having long been an *iyalocha* (female practitioner), allowing them to wash over me, losing my soul as an indescribable force took its place.

"There were once two close friends: the cat and the rat. They lived together when the world was new and things weren't always as plentiful as they are now. But the cat was an excellent hunter and the rat was an excellent cook and they lived together harmoniously.

"Then came a drought and their prey ran away and the roots of the forest dried up. All were starving including the cat's four young kittens. The cat went to the diviner for counsel. 'Don't worry,' the wise old man said. 'There are good and bad times and these hard times will soon be over. But your cousin, a leopard, is ill and needs your help. You have not seen him in a long time and when you return, things will be better.'

"'But I have four children. Will they be safe with my friend, the rat?' asked the cat. 'They will fine so long as you make *ebo* (sacrifice to the Gods),' she was told.

"The cat intended to make ebo but did not, being distracted by game that she saw and caught. She brought her catch to the rat who promised to cook it and feed the four kittens and to keep them safe while she was gone. But when the cat returned from nursing her cousin, she found only the bones and skin of her children. The famine had persisted and the rat had eaten them. The cat had not made ebo and the Gods had not protected her children. From that time on, cats have hunted and killed every rodent they find. But whose fault was it: the rat for being hungry or the cat for not making ebo?"

The letter ended with a religious phrase: "*Oho o buru, ego nii gbe ni o. Ka maa worisha.*" ("In days of turbulence, it is ebo that saves. Let us keep looking to the orisha.")

"Are you alright?" a passerby asked, looking concerned as she stood beside my car.

"Yes, thank you, I was just thinking," I said, rallying a smile.

Chapter 8

Mother Marie's advice had been vague but clear: chaos was coming and I would need aid from the Gods to survive. Being both modern and Mormon did I believe this? *Yes*, for it would be foolish not to. The Gods had saved my life twice, first from a fatal illness as a child and later from a murderer as a teenager. So, upon returning home and after checking on my children and husband, I went to a locked basement closet which held objects more valuable than money or jewels. Here, carefully wrapped in this climate-controlled room, were the herbs needed for spiritual bathing and healing, and the offerings needed to gain favor from the Gods: foods, and even tobacco in my non-smoking household.

I kept this closet locked, not from fear of theft since this would be unwarranted considering the house's modern security system but to avoid questions from my children who were too young to understand. I wanted them to have a conventional childhood even if their parents were far from that. Me, as manager of the American office of an international security company, and their father who was an already noted computer scientist. And eleven-year-old Asya, our foster child who might someday be Queen of Russia, was regarded as being merely their older sister.

That night, when all were asleep, I performed the ritual which I had too long neglected: bathing in a favored herb of my spiritual husband, Babaluaiye, In the Santeria faith, there are both bitter and sweet herbs, this referring not to their taste but to their spiritual vibrations. Sweet herbs are used to attract good luck and love and prosperity while bitter herbs are used to dispel evil. Having already achieved a bountiful family, I bathed in the bitter herb of apasote for exactly seventeen minutes, seventeen being Babaluaiye's favored number. Evil is ever present, particularly in my business.

After drying myself and dressing in a white gown, I left the bathroom for another locked room. This contained a light blue shrine holding crutches, beans, and popcorn, the icons of Babaluaiye. I prostrated myself before it with closed eyes and empty mind. For minutes there was nothing until words rumbled through me though, despite their volume, I could not say whether from within or without: *"Aye l'oja, orun n'ile. Dide died lalafia"* ("The world is a marketplace. The spirit world is home. Arise, arise in peace.").

Chapter 9

I felt better after praying, more able to cope with whatever came during this perilous time.

Worry about the COVID-19 pandemic had lessened with the production of effective vaccines. For most Americans, the experience was fading into a bad memory like the dawn can eclipse a nightmare. But for those living on the Eastern seaboard a new fright had taken its place.

A teenage volunteer at a Connecticut Congregational Church lay hospitalized in critical condition after being raped and stabbed. Three days later the body of a seven-year-old Greenwich girl, having also been stabbed and sexually assaulted, was found in the woods a hundred yards from her home. Before the shock of these crimes dispelled, a Greenwich policewoman was found lying in her patrol car, dead from two twenty-two-caliber bullets to her head, likely from a silenced pistol considering that her car stood in the Police Department parking lot.

What followed was the expected. Gun sales and shooting instruction skyrocketed with locksmiths and security companies doing a landslide business. Greenwich residents burrowed at home and streets emptied at dusk.

During this period, I also kept my children home, protected by our extensive security system, the two live-in bodyguards provided by my company, and me. I no longer considered it unseemly to walk about my home armed.

Despite his downplaying of risk, I insisted that Randy, my husband, be accompanied by an armed bodyguard on his travels. Being a gifted computer scientist who headed a startup, he had gained favorable public attention and who knew if the crime spree would turn to kidnapping. Randy accepted my demand grudgingly. Men like to think they can take care of themselves.

"My bodyguard will have big breasts, won't she?" he asked, deadpanned.

"It'll be a man," I said, without a smile.

I'm touchy about my small breasts.

Chapter 10

During times of terror it is natural for people is to turn inward, toward family and others they trust. My family had always been close though not speaking as often as I would have liked during my childhood. For some of those years my mother worked as a teacher and for most of those years my father worked long hours in his law practice. This time decreased after he closed his practice to serve as a Connecticut Supreme Court judge. Still, whenever able, I phoned my family daily, speaking with whoever happened to be at home for each had busy lives. Now having four children of my own—a baby, two toddlers, and a pre-teen foster child—I had become the mother-at-home when one of my three sisters needed to talk.

Before the recent birth of my youngest son, Adam, I tried to reduce my job tasks to the minimum since mothering chores are a full-time job no matter what anyone says. This had only been possible with help from my assistant. Jordan. A West Point graduate, he had taken on tasks ranging from marketing the business to serving as the temporary bodyguard for endangered clients. "It breaks up the routine," he said, with relish.

My conversations with my sisters consisted of the usual concerns of young adults, of which I included myself at twenty-five though feeling ancient on wearying days.

these had recently concerned crime in a town where the local newspaper's arrest blotter had ordinarily gone unread. My older sister's information was an even bigger shock.

"Have you heard?" Melody asked.

"Another killing?" I asked, touching my pistol.

"No, no," Melody said, with the tone of what is ordinarily associated with a grin.

I waited impatiently. Melody had the infuriating habit of drawing out stories.

"Okay, what is it?" I asked, giving up.

"You'll never guess."

"I won't try."

"Our father is going to Washington."

"So what? Most Americans go there sometime during their life."

"Yes, but not as a *United States senator*," she said triumphantly.

"Huh?" I exclaimed, having never outgrown this juvenile expression.

Chapter 11

"Surprised you, didn't I?" Melody asked.

"You sure did. Even more than when you were arrested," I said.

"We weren't arrested!" she objected.

"Okay, you were escorted by police cars out of town," I said.

This incident happened several years before, during a rowdy bachelorette party featuring a sexually themed float that had stopped traffic. Thereafter, her friends moved such events to anything-goes Las Vegas which is more its style.

"Our family will never forgive me," Melody said.

"I'm just teasing. It's already forgotten and we'll always love you. But what is this all about?" I asked.

"Timing and reputation. Senator Conklin is eighty-seven and has been in declining health for years. He just resigned and our dad was asked to serve the remaining four years of Conklin's term and no one objected. Which isn't surprising when considering the praise he recently got for cracking down on lawyers' fraudulent billing like the one who charged a client for a fifty-hour workday.

"I was surprised too. I thought he'd work as a lawyer all his life and his recent job as a judge made him a super-powered lawyer."

After a momentary hesitation, I shared what our father once told me. Feeling that it wasn't something he would object to my sharing with family.

"Dad never wanted to be a lawyer. He went to law school to earn a decent living after being a star debater in college. He always wanted to be a politician but married young and had a family to support. 'Achieving financial success as a politician is like being lucky enough to get a job as a well-paying shepherd,' he told me. To further quote dad, 'I wanted to graduate Harvard Law but not to practice as a lawyer.' It's just taken him a long time to get where he wanted to be."

A pregnant silence followed.

"Where will you live?" I asked.

"Who knows after our wedding next month. Greenwich? Cleveland? Wyoming?"

Greenwich, our hometown, I understood. Cleveland is home to the famed Cleveland Clinic and would be a reasonable choice considering that her fiancée is a doctor. But how did Wyoming enter the equation, I wondered.

"Why Wyoming?" I asked.

Have you watched the Netflix series, *Longmire*? About the troubles of a Wyoming sheriff today," Melody said.

"No."

"Watch it! It got rave reviews and the problems he gets into are nearly as bad as yours. My husband-to-be yearns for a family on the new frontier."

"Well, Wyoming *is* closer to Utah than Connecticut," I said.

"Please!" Melody said, with a laugh.

Unlike in Greenwich, a bachelorette float with see-through costumes and tossed condoms are unlikely to gain a friendly police escort in the staid Mormon towns of our many Utah relatives.

Chapter 12

For some inexplicable reason, after hanging up the phone my thought returned to my high school English class. Wondering what I would include in a present essay entitled, "My Summer." Certainly too little since understanding many of these events came only later. None had considered the horrors to be linked. One of the biggest jokes about life is that you learn most things too late. Yet everyone had tried.

The crime spree which began with rape and murder was quickly followed by bank robberies and the burning of inhabited churches and schools. These shattered the nation's psyche as had the COVID pandemic of the previous year.

Adding to these events was my husband's surgery and my need to care for him and the rest of my family which now included a newborn daughter, Marie.

My father's political appointment was another shock. Would my parents move to Washington and I lose their close-by support? This would be a grievous loss.

Soon after having my first children (they were twins) I learned the importance of prioritizing. Combining job demands with motherhood inevitably leaves both incomplete, which is acceptable at work but not with parenting. Even so, I had added to these priorities that of learning more about Caroline, the child who had expressed the hope to be alive when she grew up, and to check in with my parents. Would they and my younger sisters move to Washington or would my father commute, Washington being a regularly scheduled train ride on the newly spiffed Acela. I would visit them that day.

I also decided to arrange a party for my children's Montessori class in order to speak with Caroline's mother. Holding this at the home of my best friend, Erika, who, though married and a new mother, hadn't yet bought her own house. She lived with her parents on their forty-million-dollar estate to which *no one* refused an invitation. Caroline's mother would hunger to see inside. Everyone in Greenwich did.

Chapter 13

When I had asked Erika to host the party, she asked "why?".

We had long been like sisters and she sensed something was up.

"What a girl in my children's class said bothers me. When the teacher asked what she'd like to be when she grew up she replied, "alive.""

"So what. Kids say strange things, use words without realizing their meaning," Erika said.

"I know but I can't get it out of my mind. I'd never forgive myself if anything happened to her and I'd done nothing," I said, with a hint of annoyance.

"I'm sorry. I shouldn't have said that. Your instincts are better than mine. Of course I'll host the party," Erika said.

Erika was a born organizer since high school. Creating events unlike any that our classmates had seen and this party was no different. The children's addresses were happily supplied by the school and each invitation was hand-delivered within a box of *Sarah Bernhardts* from Greenwich's noted St. Moritz Pastry Shop. These chocolate-enrobed almond cookies are to die for.

Erika brushed off my apology for adding another task to her frantic schedule. "It'll break up the routine," she said, adding, "How do you plan to question the mother?"

"I hadn't thought that far ahead. Just play it by ear," I said, feeling uncomfortable, as if I had bought a horse before building their barn.

"Okay. I'll take the mothers on my standard half-hour tour to give you time to question her. How will you do it?" Erika asked.

"Not directly. It could be nothing. Kids misstate all the time," I said.

"You're going to a lot of trouble for something you only half believe," Erika said.

"I'd call it more than an anxiety and less than a fear," I said.

Erika's expression darkened.

"You have a good instinct for those things. Nature's triage is to save children first," she said.

Chapter 14

Hearing about another's life helps place ours in perspective, releasing the anxiety that can burden our soul. So I was glad to hear my oldest sister's story when she came over.

"She bought the sizzle and found there was no steak," Melody said.

I sat up straighter. This would be another of her stories from This Dating Life. One which I never had, having been with the man who became my husband since seventh grade.

"Rhea wasn't an innocent. She was twenty-five and had dated many men since being divorced two years before and was convinced he was *the one*.

"She met him at work when he came in to buy a car. The dealership didn't have exactly what he wanted and he was very precise: a high-end black BMW coupe with maroon upholstery. They had to order it, he was told that he could have it in two-weeks, and after small talk he asked her out and she accepted. He was single, thirty-three, and owned his own house, a rambling three-story near your parents.'"

"He isn't poor," I said.

"Far from it and there was a quick chemistry between them. He was romantic and easy to talk to and seemed really interested in her, sending her flowers, and buying her a diamond broach soon after they met. They walked along the beach, motored out on his yacht, rode bikes, and went to movies like an old married couple.

"'He had been married before, to a high-school sweetheart just after graduating from college. He was the only child from a rich family who spoiled him with money and whatever else he wants. They had met in April and Rhea met his family in July. They liked her since all were Methodist, and she was a serious person who had worked since she was twelve.

"They had a beautiful wedding but he changed right afterward. He insisted on controlling everything and objected when she called her family or wanted to go out with a girlfriend. His mother warned her about his moods before they married. 'Avoid him when he's in one. Don't say anything,' she said. Rhea tried her best but it simply didn't work. One morning he told her he was leaving, that the marriage was over."

"That was quite an experience. Did she learn anything from it?" I asked Melody.

"Her *best* lesson: to pay more attention to her head than to her heart."

"There'll be steak in her future. Diligence is the mother of good luck," I said.

Mothers know.

Chapter 15

When my children asked about my work, I told them that I help people to live a safe life. Did young Caroline know this? I didn't know but hoped to find out at Erika's party.

My toddler's Montessori class consisted of nine students and all showed up. Not only with their mothers but with friends of three of the mothers and their toddlers too, which Erika told them would be alright. She has a deserved reputation for kindness, and for creating notable events too.

This one was no different. Upon arriving, each child was given an animated figured box containing their costume and associated gear as a wizard or a princess or a police officer. The latter's noisy space gun proved most popular of all.

While they snacked and played, supervised by three hired babysitters, the adults explored the house. Slowly, to give me time to become acquainted with Caroline's mother who wasn't what I expected. Though well-dressed in the manner of Greenwich matrons, she lacked their typical calm. During a scheduled coffee break she continually wrung her hands as we spoke.

I opened my investigation with a neutral topic.

"I'm Margaret. Have you lived in Greenwich long?" I asked, after seating myself beside her on the sofa.

"I'm Tara. No, we just arrived from Austin," she replied.

"How do you like the town?"

"It's different."

"It sure is. My company has an Austin office so I got to know it a bit."

Getting to know someone requires sharing personal information.

"Is it a tech company?" Tara asked.

"No, my husband is into tech. I manage the American branch of an international security company," I said.

The moment of intimacy that followed was quickly withdrawn. During it, Tara had looked like an outcast, a lonely wanderer caught in a buzzsaw of intricate devious movements. Then her mask reappeared and it was gone.

Chapter 16

To relieve Tara's possible tension upon learning of my security work, I turned our conversation to the parenting worry that never stops.

"Schools are germ factories. My kids are healthy but I never stop worrying. Whooping cough was reported in Stamford. How has your daughter been?" I asked.

While this wasn't true, one should never hesitate to lie to make a helpful story more interesting.

"I didn't hear. Caroline's been healthy but maybe I should have the pediatrician check her," Tara said.

"My bodyguard was a medical doctor. She's not licensed in America but can speak with you if you're concerned. She watches my children and I trust her implicitly," I said.

"How did a doctor come to be a bodyguard?" Tara asked.

Her curiosity seemed to calm her.

"Mila has an unusual background. She's from Russia and had formerly been a doctor in the Russian military and a police officer too. My company provides security for the rich and famous. They've tried to hire her from us without success. We'll do about anything to keep an employee happy and they appreciate this. A celebrity's promises aren't to be relied on, nor are they noted for their generosity," I said.

"Hmm..." Tara murmured.

Then, apparently wanting to get more of my measure before deciding how much to reveal she asked, "Why do you need a bodyguard?"

Learning some of the perilous events in my past would have satisfied her curiosity but one should share private experiences only with intimates. I settled for a dramatic flourish. After checking that we couldn't be seen by others, I removed my Kimber Micro 9MM pistol from my shoulder bag and held it in the flat of my hand. Though small, it holds six rounds, has a laser beam, and smoothed edges for concealed carry. To reduce her shock but impress her I made a small joke.

"Life is like high school. Only the accessories change," I said, with a smile.

Chapter 17

Brandishing my pistol did shock her but her "mask" quickly descended. To maintain contact, I told her a story from my work and this had a positive effect.

"Part of being young is not knowing what you're getting into. The greatest part of my company's work is providing personal protection. I recently rented a safe house where endangered clients can temporarily remain but until then I had then stay at our home. All were congenial but having them there created so much friction with my husband that for a while I wasn't sure my marriage would survive. I do my job well and expect to CEO someday but remember what my father, the present CEO, said. 'That when you get to the top, remember that there's nothing there. The only thing that really matters is love. No matter what your accomplishments are, it's incredibly lonely if you're not surrounded by some form of love.' And he's a former army general too!" I said.

I didn't say that he had served in Russia. That unnecessary detail would have added a discordant note and pulled her further from revealing what I wanted to learn: what so upset her daughter that she feared for her life.

"Can you ever really know someone, who they *really* are? Some people are fantasists and bigger liars than journalists. They like the romance of a hidden life, the secret compensation of private power until their outer rational world and inner world collide," Tara mused, as if to herself.

I sensed that Tara's mind had switched from philosophical rambling to concern about herself. Which is what I said.

"You're not speaking hypothetically are you? Can I help?" I asked.

Tara's magnificent eyes were large, blue, and luminous, almost compelling attention from her beautiful face.

"I don't know if anyone can help me," she finally said.

Chapter 18

I stared at Tara and waited. Her beauty shone despite her paleness. She had a ripe, freely swinging body when she walked. I could imagine her drowsy look when lost in kissing. If she worked in an office, men would find excuses to go to her desk to stare at her high firm breasts. She spoke as if sensing my thoughts.

"The temporary credential of beauty can cause one to think that love is as simple as tying a string bikini while waiting for their ship to come in."

Against the backdrop of children's play, our conversation had entered a deeper level.

"Wisdom is the ability to figure out what the real issue is and focus on it. It's better to know the truth than to imagine the worst," I said.

"But what if the worst is as bad as one can imagine?" Tara asked.

"Then people hire my company," I said.

A good boss hustles for business.

"I wouldn't know what to say," Tara said.

"Whatever bothers you," I suggested.

"Nothing until last week when I had the queerest thought: that it had always seemed odd how well my husband and I fit together. Liking the same authors and movies, laughing at the same jokes, and his warm intimate manner. Does Nick really love me or is it the act of a professional who's good at it? I found myself thinking.

"As if you married a stranger," I mused.

"Exactly!"

"We are each stranger than we can imagine," I said reassuringly.

"But not a husband and wife to each other," Tara objected.

She was right.

"When did this feeling start?" I asked.

"It might always have been there, a feeling of oddness like the primal feeling that one gets after a stranger has been in one's bedroom."

"You're afraid," I said softly.

"Deathly so," Tara whispered.

Children are perceptive and I now understood her daughter's statement, that she hoped to be alive and grow up.

Chapter 19

My pesky packrat memory pawed at the shelves in the back of my mind. A place where I keep memories which I avoid thinking but can't get rid of. Like the terror I experienced while tied to a table as a sadistic monster carrying a soldering iron approached. I shook my head to lose the memory and turned toward Tara.

"Are you alright?" she asked.

"Yes. Your words aroused an unpleasant memory. Terrors can linger long after the actual fear is gone since the mind has its own schedule for forgetting. But to get back to your situation: when did you first feel uneasy about your husband?" I asked.

Tara thought silently for several moments.

"A month after we met, on a beach in Aruba. I was there with a girlfriend on a holiday from our jobs. We're civil engineers and had been working on the new water tunnel in New York City. He was walking down the beach after a sailing lesson on a sunfish, sat beside me, chatted me up, and it went from there.

"He's English but lived in America for years, working on network security for a defense contractor. Both being technical we hit it off right away. This probably wouldn't have happened if he'd been a poet except if he was *really* good looking," Tara said.

Her brief smile indicated that she was regaining control.

"That odd thing you sensed," I reminded her.

"Oh, yes. We'd been sharing our backgrounds, me in the Mid-West and he in England. He spoke of a Christmas spent with his paternal grandparents at their home in Wales. It sounded so ideal that this stuck in my mind but when I mentioned it a day later he said I must have misheard since all his grandparents died before he was born."

"Was that the only strange thing?" I asked.

Tara looked sheepish, as if she were about to reveal something too private.

"The talking in his sleep..."

I waited silently, and she continued.

"In a foreign language."

Chapter 20

"Do you remember any of the words?" I asked, though knowing only German and a little Russian.

"Just a name that was repeated: Giselle. When I asked Nick who Giselle was, he first said nothing, then that she was his childhood nanny."

"That sounds reasonable," I said supportively.

"Only if you don't know Nick. He's built like a cage fighter and has that attitude. It's lucky our only child is a girl," Tara said.

"Is there anything else?" I asked.

"Yes. A month ago, during a weekend getaway in Vienna, we were seated in the *Wiener Wiazhaus*. Do you know it?" she asked.

"Yes. It's cozy with a friendly staff and great food though too big portions," I said.

"That was my opinion too," Tara said.

She again became silent, apparently hesitant to reveal what concerned her.

"A woman came to our table. She greeted Nick as if they were old friends but he reacted coldly and said she'd made a mistake. She seemed puzzled before catching herself and agreeing but I was sure they knew each other," Tara said.

Sounds from the children's play filled the silence between us and I thought an old proverb: lies can comfort but the truth sets you free. But did she want freedom?

"Was there anything else?" I asked.

"We haven't had sex for two months if that means anything," Tara said.

"It means there's a problem. My therapist once told me that the health of a marriage can be gauged by how often the couple have sex as compared with when it was most frequent," I said.

"It he's right, our marriage is terminal," Tara said.

Chapter 21

"I feel like I've entered a *Lifetime* movie. Those where the naïve wife suspects that her husband is other than who she believed and not in a good way. The town's new business investor being an escaped mobster or a doctor being part of a drug ring," Tara said.

I felt struck by her comment, having once helped a wife who found herself in this situation.

"Though rare, it does happen. My company helped solve such a problem," I said, evenly.

"I can't say anything and what would I say? 'Tell me, exactly who are you?'"

"No, you can't," I agreed.

"What should I do?" Tara asked.

I felt uneasy, having been placed in a difficult position. Though we had met just minutes before, I liked and empathized with Tara. My job had occasionally involved extricating a person from a queasy or deadly situation. But never alone and without resources even, at times, those that I did not realize I had.

Advising Tara would change me from observer to participant which always contains peril. Moreover, not borrowing trouble was my adopted motto since enough came with my job.

Still, I felt for Tara and understood why she revealed so intimate a matter to a stranger: holding a troubling secret almost demands that you have someone to share it with. Thus I decided to give Tara helpful advice though believing that it was something she had already thought of. But maybe my action was because silence isn't always golden but can be the yellow of cowardice.

"You need to gain more information but to do so only indirectly. The woman in Austria might have been incorrect and the changes in your husband's attitude may derive from business worries or maybe one concerning health. Do you feel in danger?" I asked.

That her answer wasn't immediate gave me one.

"No," she said finally.

Her hesitancy was understandable. A woman couldn't permit herself to live with one who might harm them though many do from financial need.

"Do you have money of your own?" I asked.

"My mother was divorced twice. She impressed on her daughters the importance of financial independence, of a wife having a separate bank account. That was one lesson I learned," Tara said.

"Okay. My advice is to snoop quietly. Check for curiosities in what your husband says, like his comments about his grandfather and not knowing the woman. Hide your real feelings by talking about ordinary stuff like your day with Caroline. I'll give you my cellphone number. Call me each day before 10:00AM to check in with me," I said.

My advice produced the expected reaction.

"You sound worried," Tara said, with a fearful edge.

"People are nice until they aren't," I said.

My casual tone didn't reassure her. Instead, she looked at me intently.

"My mother might have been air-mailed from Hell except for giving me that same good advice," she said softly.

Chapter 22

"Do you feel uneasy about helping me?" Tara asked.

"A bit. Why do you ask?"

"Because not being scared would mean you were too stupid to help me," she said.

It was one of those hours when imagination lends wings, when the difficult is easy and the dubious is certain.

"You're right. So tell me something else your frightful mother gave you," I said, with a smile.

"Do you know about the Magi in the Book of Matthew?" she asked.

"The three wise men who gave tribute to the baby Jesus," I said.

As the product of a fourth-generation Mormon family which attended church religiously (an old pun), I would be expected to. But I merely said, "Yes."

"They were reported to be able to do magic, like my mother and I can," Tara said.

I stared. Our earlier conversation had been like a verbal meringue: mostly air with nothing solid inside but this statement caught me short. Religions are mystical to varying degree with the same act being considered religious or magic depending on where it is carried out. Praying for rain in a church is considered *religious* but chanting and dancing for the same outcome is deplored as *magic*.

Africa-based religions are belittled by being termed Voodoo cults with connotations of zombies, sticking pins in dolls, and sorcerers using children's blood in ritual killings. But Santeria believes in good witchcraft too and I wondered which Tara referred to.

"Tell me more," I said evenly.

"Don't consider me crazy," she said.

"I won't. I've heard unbelievable stories that turned out to be true," I said, feeling lost in her personality despite my instinctive common sense.

"It *is* true," she said simply.

Then she told me.

Chapter 23

"My father loved chocolate chip pancakes not only for breakfast but anytime," Tara began, pausing to wipe tear-filling eyes.

"I loved them too but my mother never did. She was a health-nut and said they weren't healthy."

I pondered where her story was going but didn't say anything, wondering for the first time if she was crazy and her child's fear reflected growing up in a weird family. Perhaps sensing my disbelief, Tara explained.

"I'm getting there. It'll all make sense," she promised.

I waited.

"My father love of chocolate-chip pancakes began their last argument. He wanted breakfast at the Pancake House, she didn't want me to go, and he stormed out the door and from our lives. We could have gone with him and had a different meal but there was more to it. The night before my mother had a nightmare about eating pancakes in a restaurant. We'd all ordered them but the maple syrup that we poured turned out to be blood which spread from the pancakes all over us and the room.

"My mother felt this symbolized being murdered at a restaurant but my father dismissed this. Next morning he went out to eat by himself and became one of the seven victims of *The Pancake Massacre.* Media always seem to find a catchy phrase for the most awful horror. So my mother's magic saved our lives. Had we accompanied my father we would have been killed too."

"Does your mother have other gifts?" I asked.

"Yes. Ever since childhood she had the ability to touch an object and tell things about its owner. A hundred years ago she might have been in vaudeville and a hundred years earlier been burned as a witch," Tara said.

I waited, sensing that more was coming.

"My mother phoned me last week, after she dreamt that I had been murdered," Tara said.

Chapter 24

I began feeling like I was groping in a dark unfamiliar room filled with odd odors and awkward pieces of furniture. Having felt death to be imminent creates a bonding experience. Tara now feared this and I had experienced it in the past.

"Did your mother say more?" I asked.

"No."

"You said that you had magical powers too. Can you sense anything?" I asked.

Maybe," Tara said slowly.

I waited.

"Yesterday morning, when Nick was in the bathroom. I went through his wallet looking for I don't know what. I didn't find anything odd but touching it gave me a sense that he would soon be gone from my life," Tara said.

I waited for more but there was none. Just as a picture puzzle can't be completed when pieces are missing, I couldn't be sure of anything without having more facts. Our unease might not be justified since the explanations could be ordinary: there were problems in the marriage, the woman in the restaurant who Nick denied knowing was a past lover, and the reduced intimacy was further evidence of this couple's need for a marital counselor rather than an investigator. But should a life stake on this degree of uncertainty?

"Would you like my company to check Nick's background, to see if it hangs together?" I asked.

"What would this cost?" Tara asked.

"Nothing. We do pro bono work like lawyers and your job wouldn't take long. You could have our report in a few days, then decide if more is needed," I said.

"Thank you. For me and Caroline, and maybe Nick too," Tara said.

I glanced at the children and understood their raised voices. The sight of St. Moritz Pastry Shop's scrumptious cookies tends to have that effect.

Chapter 25

Trouble never seems to come one-at-a-time for a mother and juggling motherhood with career makes them worse.

Soon after my father's appointment as a United States senator, he and my mother decided to move to Washington along with my two younger sisters. Melody, my older sister, would soon be married and out the family nest as one might say.

"To do a good job I'll have to live there," my father explained.

His tone was apologetic but we understood. Living the bachelor life during the week and commuting to Greenwich for weekends (and maybe not all of them either) wasn't what my mother signed up for or either of them wanted. I had no right to object though I and my children would miss them. Which would also happen if my career mandated a move to Europe as seemed likely in the future.

Just as I was becoming accustomed to this change and my work-life heated up, my husband, Randy, became the focus of my attention. Illness does this, forcing one's attention on what is really important.

Randy's spurious medical complaints were legendary in my family. Since childhood he feared the sight of blood, was terrified of injections, and had fainted during my first childbirth, thereafter remaining in the waiting room during my later deliveries. Now he was the patient.

That I initially hadn't been attentive to his grumbling was understandable though not excusable. I should have known better since even hypochondriacs do get sick and not only in their head. Many wives also complain about their husband not listening. It was his father, a physician, to whom he had earlier revealed all his symptoms.

Chapter 26

"Both the MRI and CT scans found an acoustic neuroma," Randy said casually, in response to his father's question about the findings from his exams.

"*What*?" I asked, giving Randy a hard stare.

"The dizziness I complained about. Dad referred me to an otolaryngology specialist and that's what he said," Randy replied.

Anger and fear swept over me: anger that he hadn't shared this with me first and fear of its nature. Pushing down these emotions I asked calmly, "What is it?"

"An acoustic neuroma, which is also called a vestibular schwannoma, is a rare non-cancerous growth that develops on the eighth cranial nerve. This nerve runs from the inner ear to the brain and is responsible for hearing and balance. Typical symptoms are ringing in the ears, imbalance, and dizziness with a hearing loss being the initial symptom for most people," Randy's father said.

"I noticed that recently," Randy said evenly.

His calm amazed me since, like I said, Randy was known to faint at the sight of blood and tremble before vaccinations. But perhaps I shouldn't have been surprised since he tended to pull himself together and handle true emergencies well. Government agencies and corporations relied on him to resolve system-wide computer catastrophes. I regained control, saw that the children were engaged in a typical squabble, and spoke calmly.

"How worried should we be?" I asked, addressing Randy's father.

"Though these tumors are non-cancerous and grow slowly, they should be treated quickly. The cause is unknown and there are apparently no risk factors. Randy wasn't exposed to those that were studied, loud occupational noise and cancer-treatment radiation. It usually occurs more in women than men and is rare in children. The decision to make now is whether to do *watchful waiting* or remove the tumor with microsurgery."

Into the silence that followed, I asked, "What do you advise?"

Chapter 27

"Since all surgery involves risk, watchful waiting is a good choice. The decisive factor is how much the problem affects your life. It's not potentially fatal like a quickly growing cancer," Randy's father said.

"Randy travels a lot. There could be a serious accident if he got dizzy while getting off a plane or on an escalator," I said, shying away from the word *fatal*.

"There's that," Randy's father agreed.

Now, for the first time since we met many years before, I liked and felt a closeness with him. Randy and I began dating in the seventh grade, which was when his father's objection to me began. Not personally since my family was well-respected in Greenwich but because his goal for Randy was a medical career and I would be a distraction. Which I had been by involving him in my personal crises and expanding the horizon of his life.

Randy had rejected a medical career, becoming a noted computer expert after earning a doctorate from Columbia University. Now the fact of his parents' love for him really hit me, as it should have long before and I have for my children. I would sacrifice my life for them, as Randy's parents would for him.

Silence filled the table as Randy decided.

"Margaret is right. Even slight dizziness, which can occur suddenly, is a big risk. I'll have the surgery," he said.

None of us responded, knowing that every medical intervention and particularly those involving anesthesia is risky. But Randy was young and healthy.

That night we lay in bed, trying to comfort each other. The sadness in the room was overwhelming. When you genuinely love someone, you fall in love again and again.

Chapter 28

The only thing worse than waiting for *your* diagnosis is waiting for the medical outcome of someone you love. By pulling strings, Randy's father arranged the surgery with a famed surgeon the following week. We only told the children that daddy would be away for a few days, which was a familiar event. Years before, when Randy lived during the week in graduate student housing in Manhattan, they named him their "traveling daddy."

Surprisingly, despite Randy's long fear of medical procedures, he was calm as I drove him to the hospital. This might have been caused by the reassuring comment of the surgeon's nurse when we first met. "He's a God," she said reassuringly of her boss.

Though hoping to be alone with my worry, the hospital's waiting room was packed and I found myself seated beside a worried man. His wife was giving birth to their first child, she was small, and he was terrified. Despite my own troubling situation, I found myself being supportive by sharing the healthy outcomes of my childbirths. When he asked why I was there, I told him, violating my rule of not sharing intimate matters with strangers.

But medical settings tend to make its inhabitants comrades, I thought.

Helping this expectant father helped me too since the time seemed to fly. The surgeon's approach was announced by the sound of the opening door.

"The tumor is out. Your husband is now normal or as normal as he'd ever been," he said, with the smile of a winner.

"How will his hearing and balance be?" I asked, shakily.

"*Absolutely normal*! Do I do miracles or do I do miracles?" he joked.

Feeling like I had received a last-minute reprieve from a death sentence, I acted as I avoid doing in public though there's nothing wrong with it. I cried.

Chapter 29

Before Randy was discharged from the hospital, I asked the surgeon for advice.

"Randy has been through a lot. What can I do to help him?"

Before answering, the doctor offered me coffee which I declined, without explaining that Mormons don't drink it. Lecturing others and particularly doctors about their diet isn't my style. After several sips, the doctor began what seemed a well-rehearsed lecture.

"Just as people need a physiological homeostasis or equilibrium, they also require a sense of social and psychological equilibrium, behaving in a characteristic way. When something upsets their usual balance, they try things to restore it. A major change in their life creates a crisis, a period of disorganization accompanied by fear and anxiety and maybe even guilt.

"A person can't remain in extreme distress for long so every crisis is brief with the new balance being healthy and indicating psychological growth, or unhealthy and representing psychological deterioration. The illness that Randy experienced was such a crisis but he made a good decision and is being returned to his family healthier than he was though with marks.

"You have told me of his hypochondriacal streak and this may become worse, or better now that he's surmounted a real medical crisis. I would expect him to be more empathic with the pains and worries of others, and more likely to speak of them. I'll see him once a month for the next two months, not from medical concern but to provide reassurance for the unwarranted worries he may have. You can sit in if you like but it may be best for us to speak alone. Of course you should feel free to call me anytime."

"I'm so grateful," I said quickly, tearing up at his kindness.

"It's deserved. Years ago, your dad helped me out with a legal problem. And now he'll be a United State senator."

"The family will be moving to Washington next month. I'm not looking forward to it," I said, veering into a personal matter.

"You'll handle it well but I do have a question. I do a weekly Grand Rounds at Columbia- Presbyterian Hospital in Manhattan and don't feel secure in the present situation. Can your company provide me with a bodyguard on the days that I'm there?"

Chapter 30

I was both shocked by Doctor Ellis' request. While supplying bodyguards had been my company's main service when it began, this was during Russia's Wild West days immediately after the fall of Communism. As life gradually became safer, our bodyguard service there became confined to the ultra-rich, celebrities, and foreign diplomats. That ordinary New Yorkers now felt this need made me sad, but glad that we could help too.

"We've long provided this service here and abroad. Give me your schedule and I'll make the arrangements. You'll be traveling in an armored SUV with two former Special Forces soldiers. You can describe them as relatives that you're showing around the city," I said.

"That sounds expensive," Doctor Ellis said.

"There won't be a charge. Like lawyers, we also do pro bono work. Consider it our gift to the medical community," I said.

Though heartfelt, I reminded myself that I did run a business. This was my second such gesture in the past month and had better be my last for a while. Good public relations doesn't pay employee salaries.

"You're like your father," Doctor Ellis said, admiringly.

"He taught me well. I try to be," I said.

I smiled and left quickly, sensing that my generosity had made him uncomfortable. But personal bodyguard services are expensive. Could Doctor Ellis afford our usual fee of two-thousand-dollars a day? He could for a short time but not for many months. Nor was it fair for him to have to pay this since his Grand Rounds was a volunteer service.

Upon returning home, my bodyguard, Mila, grabbed me.

"*Have you heard?*" she asked, impatiently.

"Is it the children?" I asked worriedly.

"No, they're fine but you and Randy should no longer travel unescorted. The Chase Bank in town was just robbed. Its manager and four employees were killed."

Chapter 31

Greenwich has long been celebrated as peaceful, a family-oriented town causing newcomers seeking nightspots to move elsewhere. It's boring but in a nice way with great schools, police officers wearing white gloves while directing traffic and knowing passersby, and children with courtesy drummed into them.

No elderly person can carry packages along our main street, Greenwich Avenue, without being asked if they need help. Thus the local crime wave came as a shock to the town's collective soul. Were it a hundred years before, townspeople in droves would volunteer to police the streets. Now they cowered at home, as all did during the COVID pandemic but with guns at hand.

"What happened?" I had asked Mila.

"The typical dumbness of bank robbers though even more this time. These crimes make no sense since the haul is usually small and the prison time is long once caught which typically happens. Killings are rare since all that need be done after passing a note to a terrified teller is to collect the money and run. But here they entered the bank soon after it opened, placed a closed sign on the door, sprayed the security video lenses with shaving foam, and cleaned out the vault. The slaughter was unnecessary," she said, vehemently.

"I almost wish we were moving to Washington with my parents," I said.

"No, you're better off here. Horrors like this are frequent there."

Which was true since Greenwich is *far* safer according to statistics. Still, the internet had recently filled with stories of startling murders, robberies, and hijacked computer systems. The world is falling apart, I thought as I hugged my baby.

Chapter 32

I couldn't stop thinking that the world was cratering though this might have been simply another *mother thing,* like ordering children to look both ways when crossing the street even if it's a horse path (some ride horses on our country roads). And possibly because a move is another *mother thing,* my parents' move to Washington soon overlain my concern with safety.

Despite the booming suburban real estate offers brought on by the pandemic, my parents had refused to sell their home for sentimental and practical reasons. Since the senatorial term to which my father was appointed had four-years before the next election, many things could happen. He might stand for re-election and lose or choose to retire, deciding that he had done enough public service as a judge and senator. Having a home to return to gave my parents flexibility and maintained family roots. My oldest, newly married sister and her husband might live there while he became established in his medical practice and she attended law school.

Quickly, too quickly it seemed for such a huge change, my parents and younger sisters were gone. Leaving me with a feeling of emptiness that I tried filling with compulsive work.

I faced my assistant, Jordan, in the conference room of my company's downtown office. Which I frequented only for occasional meetings with clients, and Jordan's weekly sharing of problems for decisions that I need make.

"Our new security venture is booming. More people now want protection when traveling," he said.

"Do we have too much staff? I'd hate to have to lay off people once things are back to normal," I said.

"I haven't hired anyone permanently. The Greenwich Police Department gave me a list of retired officers who would be interested in occasional work and some of our bodyguards would like the extra income. It's easy work," he added.

"Until it isn't," I said, still having the bank's killing spree in mind.

Chapter 33

Since my father's appointment as a senator became known, visiting my family had become an obstacle course. Needing to barrel past reporters waiting outside, all hoping for a scoop on how he *really* was. Not as a somber former judge but something exciting, like being drunk by 7PM when he began beating his wife and children. Hopefully with video as good as that created by the Texas teenager being spanked by her father as he unknowingly faced her phone's camera. But the only film these reporters got were of my children being typically troublesome as I hustled them into my parents' home.

Asya, the foster child who lived with us, was the real star. Since the local murder of parents and the discovery of her heritage as a descendant of Russia's Romanov royal family, her notoriety was guaranteed. Americans love royalty and Asya's beauty and history entranced all. But she handled crowds as if she were born to the task or had been so trained by her deceased (diplomat) father, granting them a smile and wave but not a word.

We had grown to love Asya who was now a permanent part of our family. Regarded as a big sister by our younger children and with my parents becoming her courtesy grandparents. Loss had become so much a part of her life that she seemed unable to believe in a continuing relationship. When I remarked this to my mother she said, "Give her time. She's been through s lot," which was certainly true. Learning her possible destiny as Russia's future queen after the murder of her adoptive parents would be too much for any child, even one as gifted as she.

So maybe I shouldn't have been surprised that it was Asya, at my parents' home before they left for Washington, who had clearly understood what the nation was experiencing.

Chapter 34

"Have you read the old-time English writers?" I asked Jordan.

"A few in high school," he replied with a puzzled look since my question was far from what we had been speaking of.

"There's a famous 18th century series of novels, *The Life and Opinions of Tristram Shandy, Gentleman*, by Lawrence Sterne. I hated reading them in high school but one of Sterne's lines stuck in my mind and I looked it up to get it right. 'It is the nature of the hypothesis when once a man has conceived it that it assimilates everything to itself as proper nourishment and from the first moment of begetting it generally grows stronger by everything you see, hear, read or understand.'"

"Okay," Jordan said slowly.

"I can't stop thinking of Asya's statement: that the current rush of horrifying, apparently unrelated crimes are connected in some way," I said.

"She's young and has been through a lot" Jordan said.

"Yes, but she's also very smart and was brought up by a diplomat. She said there *must be* an underlying motive to these crimes, that they were leading to something bigger. An event that we would miss predicting because we were being sidetracked to concentrate on the fallen leaves and not the soon-to-fall tree."

I waited before speaking further, wanting Jordan to take seriously what Asya had said and I believed.

"Did she say anything else?" he asked.

"Yes. She said that the creator of these acts was an ambush predator, like an animal who kills with lightning speed before vanishing."

"If she's right then the police will have a big job ahead," Jordan said.

"Not just the police but the federal government too," I said.

Chapter 35

Randy dropped our local newspaper, the *Greenwich Times,* onto the floor, ignoring my scolding glance since this set a bad example for our watching children.

"Today seems a rare example of something being worse than the newspapers are reporting," he said.

"What happened?" I asked, nervously.

"A butchering, now in Virginia. An entire family was cut to pieces and posed in their bedrooms. The police consider it the act of a murder cult, like those of California's Manson Family gang fifty years ago. One of their victims, Sharon Tate, was eight-and-a-half months pregnant."

"Anyone want more cereal?" I asked, quickly changing the subject.

I held my tongue though speaking of this hadn't been one of Randy's better parental moments. For a marriage to survive each spouse must choose their battles and Randy *was* a good father. Fear had caused him to impulsively raise this matter, the same fear that had been spreading across America like the COVID virus. It was as if as quickly as one crisis departed, another rose to take its place. I yearned for Greenwich's return to the tranquil boredom that I had hungered to flee as a teenager.

My four-year-old son had taken to carrying his space pistol everywhere, delighting in startling the unaware with its noise. I understood that its attraction derived from a child's normal fear of being small in an adult world, or possibly their sensing of the fear experienced by his parents. I raised my hands in surrender when becoming the target. "Yes, sir, Mr. Sheriff," I exclaimed to his delight.

A few days later Randy's suggestion changed our lives.

"I'll be spending a lot of time in Washington next year. Why don't we move there temporarily like your parents did?" he asked.

Chapter 36

Could I move to Washington? I asked myself. Being the local manager of my company, I had the power to decide. But would I be as effective a boss if situated elsewhere? I raised this question with Erika, who is a co-manager of her father's hedge fund and my long best friend.

"There's nothing keeping you here. Your assistant, Jordan, works independently, his wife does much of the paperwork now, and he can phone if there's a problem. And you'll make great business contacts in Washington so your CEO would applaud the move," she said.

"Now you know why I asked you," I said.

"To give you the answer you wanted?" Erika asked, with a smile.

"No, because you're the cleverest person that I know," I said.

"When people compliment me I know they want something," Erika said, and we both smiled.

"We'll FaceTime with our babies. I want them to know each other growing up," she said.

"Absolutely. And maybe marry someday too," I said.

We laughed again, this being one of our old jokes, we having long been as close as sisters.

Despite Erika's considered advice and our good relationship with my parents, I wasn't sure the move would work. When considering Washington's terrible traffic, forcing Randy to endure a daily commute from bordering Virginia or Maryland wouldn't do. And the large house required by our two adults, four children and two bodyguards, would be hard to find quickly in the city.

I solved this dilemma by renting the largest available apartment at the Watergate, the complex that played a prominent role in former President Nixon's downfall. I hoped this wouldn't provide a gloomy omen for my family too.

Chapter 37

"There are no perfect family decisions," Erika reassured me after I grumbled.

While the logistics of our Washington move went well, settling into the apartment proved complicated not that I hadn't anticipated it. Still, I might have been mesmerized by the Watergate's glamour for its past tenants included Justice Ruth Bader Ginsburg, Elizabeth Taylor, and Monica Lewinsky. But when all was said and done and though our apartment was the largest available, it was really too small. The four bedrooms were a stretch for four adults (Randy, me, two live-in bodyguards) and four children.

"Have the older kids consider it a camping trip by using sleeping bags, tents, and flashlights," Erika suggested.

"I *hate* camping," I rejoined crossly.

"Whatever," Erika said, giving up.

But that's what I did and it worked. Randy, me, and the baby took one bedroom, ten-year-old Asya was given the second bedroom, the two toddlers were given their bedroom, and the two female bodyguards shared the largest bedroom. Each bedroom had an adjoining bathroom, there also being a half-bathroom located by the front door which had a private elevator entrance. For an adult needing to escape the hubbub, the large balcony was available.

Outside were swimming pools and acres of landscaped gardens with views of the river. The real estate agent had boasted of the complex' Christmas parties, which the kids would love but the armed bodyguards who I would insist accompany them might not be permitted.

While relaxing in bed one night, Randy said approvingly, "You did a good job. The move worked out well,"

"Yes, it has," I said, snuggling close.

But I had *really* wanted a separate room for my home-office rather than using a screened-off corner of our bedroom.

Chapter 38

Nothing exciting happened during our first weeks in the nation's capital. Leaving my baby with Mila (my personal bodyguard, informal medical advisor, and emergency babysitter), I often explored our neighborhood.

The Watergate is a luxurious, self-contained community where residents can work, live, and relax. The park-like landscaping contains gardens, fountains, and a shopping area that includes a post office, medical and dental offices, a drugstore, restaurants, a bakery and a grocery.

It has 24/7 concierge service, a front desk and doorman, and a parking garage. There is a walking and jogging trail, and three shopping centers are only a three- or four-minute drive, as are the Lincoln Memorial and National Geographic Museum. Despite having no reason to fret I did, and for reasons that I considered childish even before Erika agreed.

"Nothing is permanent except change," she said cautiously.

"I know but maybe some changes come too quickly. Moving to a new city, my parents being too swamped with obligations to drop-in, and Randy coming home late every night, worn-out and just wanting sleep, I feel like I'm drowning. And James insisted on sleeping with me last night, saying he was afraid to sleep alone," I said.

"You haven't had a good week," Erika said, sympathetically.

It takes another mother to understand, I thought.

"Let's deal with one thing at a time. What did you tell James?" Erika asked.

"Just what our therapists told us years ago. That dreams are our friends and like mystery movies which must be figured out. That a scary dream can't hurt you but is just telling you that something scares you, maybe because you're learning something new like how to ride a bike," I said.

"Did it work?" Erika asked.

"I'll see tonight, laying in his bed until he falls asleep. I'm getting little enough sex from Randy even without our little intruder," I said.

"Are you *serious*?"

"Randy has become a very busy figure in Washington," I said.

Chapter 39

"Huh!" Erika exclaimed, being momentarily at a loss for words. "It'll get better," she said finally.

"Or worse," I said gloomily.

To change the subject, she asked, "How's your business going?"

"Great, except for being too busy. We're a small company and with the increase in crime, demand is exceeding our resources. Now everyone seems to feel the need for a bodyguard, which is good for our business but not as an indicator of where society is going," I said.

As the silence between us lengthened, a worrying job offer popped into my mind. My speaking with Erika had likely aroused it since if wisdom is the ability to figure out the real issue and what to do, she is one of the wisest people I know. And trustworthy too since whatever I tell her she will keep to the grave, to use a dark metaphor.

"Can I ask your help with another problem?" I asked, though knowing the answer.

"Do you have to ask?"

"Of course not but it's a *really* crazy one," I said.

"I've heard them all. Rich people can be weird," Erika said.

"You haven't heard one like this," I said, and told her.

"A man offered one of my employees ten-thousand-dollars just for listening to his proposal. He did and got the money but threw the decision whether to accept back to me," I said."

"For that kind of money the guy must want someone murdered," Erika said.

I stifled a laugh and Erika asked, "What?"

"You're right, he does," I said.

"Tell me the whole story," Erika said slowly.

I did.

Chapter 40

"Josef, one of our bodyguards, is a former Russian Special Forces soldier. He was nursing his vodka in a Greenwich bar and thinking about his ex when he noticed a man staring at him. The man approached and said he had a proposition for him to consider. My employee is a good-looking blond who had been erroneously hit on before by gay men so he just said he wasn't interested and turned back to his drink. But the guy persisted, said it had nothing to do with sex and that he'd pay him ten-thousand-dollars to listen to his offer and much more if he'd agree.

"This got Josef's attention. He agreed to listen and was given an address to go to the next night. Josef did, armed and accompanied by his best friend, another bodyguard who would listen via Josef's phone while waiting in the car.

"The house was a huge Georgian mansion. The name on the mailbox, Clinton Lionel Dupray, was of a well-publicized member of Greenwich's social elite. Upon seeing this, Josef relaxed and knocked. Clinton opened the door, invited him in, and led him to his home office where he offered him a drink which Josef declined and a pack of hundred-dollar bills that he accepted.

"What do you want done?" Josef asked.

"In exchange for payment of an additional two-hundred-thousand-dollars, I want you to kill me," Clinton said.

"Josef stared as Clinton continued. 'I'm logical, not mad. I suffer from incurable pancreatic cancer and will die an excruciating death within two months which I want to avoid. I look wealthy (he said this with an expansive wave of his arms) but am broke and the CEO of a dying company. My family will be penniless when I'm dead. My twenty-million-dollar accident insurance policy has a double-indemnity clause if I die because of homicide but will pay nothing if it's caused by illness. It's a cheap policy that I bought long ago and never looked at until now. It's my only policy. I'm young and thought that I'd live forever.

"To earn the payment you must make my murder look like it happened during a robbery. I've created the plan and gotten the pistol. You'll come here on a night when the family and housekeeper are out. There'll be no danger to you. Consider it a good deed, and a well-paid one too,'" Clinton said.

Chapter 41

"What do you think?" I asked Erika.

"What do I think?" she repeated, rhetorically. "That the guy is crazy or crazy like the proverbial fox. What did Josef reply?" she asked.

"He said that he'd think about it and they're to meet in a week. What should I advise Josef?" I asked.

This response was longer in coming.

"Two-hundred-thousand-dollars is a lot of money but you have a hunch that Josef won't live to spend it," Erika said.

A moment later adding, "No, wait! Tell Josef that more information is needed, that he needs time to learn if Clinton really is dying and his finances. Say you're leery of good deeds with a benefit but not a burden and let me know what turns up, Clinton's proposal is the most fascinating that I've ever heard."

"Do you have time to hear another?" I asked.

"It would make my year," Erika said.

"Do you remember Caroline, the girl in my kids' Montessori class?" I asked.

"The one who said she wanted to be *alive* when she grew up?"

"Yes. Her anxiety may simply reflect her mother's, she having a husband who doesn't seem quite kosher. A woman addressed him by another name in a tavern."

"That's not good," Erika said.

"No. I had told her that my company would check out her husband pro bono and now added Josef's problem to that list," I said.

"Your CEO won't be happy with doing work for free," Erika said.

"It'll only take a few hours of our time and who knows what'll turn up?"

"Like six years ago in Berlin," she said, with a smile.

"Just so," I said.

There, Randy and I had secured our financial future by stealing a crook's ill-gotten gains.

Chapter 42

"Why do you want to help them?" Erika asked.

"That's a good question. I don't really know. Maybe because they're baffled, as I've felt at times in my life. Helping them is like re-living my life but in a better way."

"And maybe because helping them as you were helped," Erika suggested.

"Yes, there had always been someone watching out for me wherever I was, though I didn't know it at the time," I admitted.

"What's happening in Greenwich?" I asked, feeling a longing for home and hoping not to learn of another crime.

"The economy is booming again and realtors are calling with unreal offers. Just a few years ago Greenwich was considered to have the worst housing market in the country. It got so bad that the town hired a public relations firm to improve its image from that of white and snobbish to cultured and diverse.

"Wealthy COVID-fleeing Manhattanites flocked to Greenwich, wanting large houses with home-offices and swimming pool. They first rented but as remote working dragged on they bought and enrolled their children in local schools. Formerly, buyers wanted to be close to downtown but now huge estates in back country Greenwich are selling, those that had been hard to sell because of their size."

"Greenwich's private schools and country clubs has always made it a bedroom community for rich Manhattanites," I said.

"More so now. Tommy Hilfiger's house is being sold," Erika said.

I had visited the fashion mogul's French Normandy-style estate during a charity tour. The nearly fourteen-thousand-foot house had six bedrooms, six fireplaces, a screening room, and a wine cellar. There were formal gardens, fountains, a swimming pool, a tennis court, and a guesthouse.

"Your house could be in contract within a week," Erika said.

"I will *never* permanently leave Greenwich. My son will marry your daughter in my garden," I said firmly.

We both laughed, this having been our joke since her child was born.

Chapter 43

My childhood wasn't typical for wealthy Greenwich. While in elementary school, my father became ill with Lyme Disease and our family descended into poverty. Our meals were enabled by Food Stamps, the Mormon Food Bank, and local farmers for whom my father provided free legal services before being forced to close his practice. My clothes were hand-me-downs from my older sister and vacation travel became a thing of the past. While my father eventually recovered and returned to work, the experience of being poor had seared me and I vowed that my children would never experience it. Not if I and their father could help it, that is.

Having been fortunate we could and took our children on educational trips to the usual sites. Now, never having seen our nation's capital, I and our four children explored it, accompanied by two bodyguards in the armored SUV that was another of my company's perks.

I had asked the Watergate concierge for a tour guide and Thomas, a retired, ex-Senate aide, was recommended. During the getting-to-know-you in my apartment, I quickly realized his value. Thomas was not only knowledgeable about Washington monuments but of the city itself.

"We'll look at the White House grounds, the guards at their kiosks and driveway that curves up the entrance and be impressed with the city's majesty. Until we've driven into the heart of Washington which resembles a sick bay containing every disease affecting the body politic: selfishness, ineptitude, foolishness, deceit, and envy in their purest form with political con artists preying on their fellow man.

"Metropolitan Washington is really three cities. The largest consists of federal employees who live in the suburbs and commute. They are well paid, well educated, and never face layoffs.

"The second group, the movers and shakers, is *official* Washington, the bureaucrats who make policy. These are the cocktail-party power elite who are in the city but never part of it.

"The last group are the poor inner-city residents whose only contact with federal office buildings is when they clean them. The city of Washington is their biggest employer in a place where there are mostly only service jobs left. The schools in the suburbs are among the best in the nation but those in the inner city are among the worst with abysmal test scores and a huge dropout rate. Local politicians play racial politics and steal everything that isn't nailed down, using the White Establishment as scapegoat for the city's troubles.

"In short, the local leaders are demagogues and thieves, the public schools and hospitals are dreadful, and huge public funds have been squandered or stolen. Washington has the most crooked and incompetent urban government in America."

I sat stunned by his torrent of words.

"Is it even worth taking a tour of the city?" I asked.

"Of course," Thomas said assuredly, with a big smile. "Many of its buildings are lovely."

Chapter 44

Thanks to Thomas' acidic observations, our two-hour drive was less tiresome than I had imagined. It would have been better to leave my baby home but, like all mothers of newborns, I felt uneasy when he was out of sight. So I had brought him along, to doze in a well-constructed carryall strapped to the seat while the older children and I viewed the sights under Thomas' tutelage.

"May I ask an indelicate question?" he asked.

"Of course."

"Why are we traveling armed?"

"I thought you might ask. I manage the American office of an international security company and the CEO insists on it. It wouldn't be good publicity for their executive to be mugged. He's also my father," I said.

"What company is that?" Thomas asked.

I told him.

"Isn't that a Russian company?" he asked.

"My father is a retired Russian general living in Berlin but the company is international. Our London office is managed by a former British spy and we have retired CIA officials on our board. We provide protective services for celebrities and Western government officials," I said.

"You do semi-military work too. Rescuing those sex slaves in the Baltic gained your company good publicity," Thomas said.

"And praise too," I said, always being the hustling business manager.

"Deservedly so."

In the silence that followed my toddler daughter fussed and I drew her close.

"What is your company's fee?" Thomas asked suddenly.

"That depends on the job," I said.

"Of course," he said abruptly. Then, as if being embarrassed by his tone, he added, "It's for a personal matter."

"Our fees are individual and those from our wealthy clients allow us to do pro bono work too. Can you give me a sense of the trouble?" I asked.

"My daughter has gone crazy. She's infatuated with a crook," Thomas said.

Chapter 45

"Because every woman wants to be first in someone's life explains many of the strange things that they do," I said.

"Even with an evil man?" Thomas asked.

"Sometimes. How old is your daughter?" I asked.

"She's twenty-four."

A grown-up, I thought. The same might have happened with me had I a different family.

"Tell me about it," I said.

His story was slow in coming, not being what any parent wants to share.

"Cora, Dakota's mother, was never strong. She took to alcohol as a teenager, achieving sobriety only after seven rehabs. We met during our last year in college. She studied art and I studied economics. We began living together and her earnings as a model helped pay my law school expenses. I later realized how well her personality fit with modeling," Thomas said, and paused.

"Because models are beautiful outside and empty within. Beauty is a temporary credential," I suggested.

"You've known models," he said, a wry smile softening his face as he continued.

"Conceiving wasn't easy for Cora. She had two miscarriages before Dakota was born and the doctor said her birth was a miracle. We loved Dakota but Cora wasn't good at mothering. Dakota would run to me, be a daddy's girl, and Cora resented this. Not by what she said but in her attitude which kids can sense. I brought in an au pair, Cora returned to modeling, and we were a happy family or so I thought.

"I had been politically active in college and took a term off to work on a senator's successful campaign. This paid off and my first job after law school was as political assistant in that senator's office. I've worked in Washington ever since.

"I don't regret the long working hours but my family suffered. I was the emotional parent for both Cora and Dakota and wasn't there when they needed me. You can imagine what happened."

"Cora returned to drinking and Dakota took up with a low-life," I said.

"You've dealt with this before," Thomas said.

"It's the lifecycle of many of our celebrity clients," I said.

"Can you help us? Bring Dakota back?" Thomas asked.

We both knew that he was asking the near impossible: to wrest an adult from a lover she had tied herself to to and bring her home. Moreover, his family couldn't afford our fee so this would be my office's third pro bono case and raise concern. But if we succeeded, Thomas might be an excellent referral source for future private and government work.

His problem was worth the try. Instinct can defy logic and accomplish an apparently impossible task, I told myself.

Chapter 46

"How was your day?" Randy asked.

I and the kids had just returned home, feeling exhausted. A child's energy can seem inexhaustible but all were asleep within minutes of arriving home. Even Asya who had greater stamina than many adults.

"Draining," I said, dropping onto the sofa beside him.

"You work too hard," Randy said, empathetically.

"Told by one compulsive worker to another."

"I have one job but you have two. Being a mother is a full-time job and we don't need the money."

We didn't, being among America's financially comfortable families, a status which would rise when Randy's start-up went public. Even Erika's father, who went from a math professorship to create a successful hedge fund, was impressed. His banking contact would handle the initial public offering of Randy's company.

"I took on another pro bono case," I said casually.

I felt free to share my business secrets with Randy, knowing that he would never break confidence. Holding secrets almost demands that you have someone to share them with. Yet I wondered why I chose to share *this* job detail since I usually didn't. Was I so exhausted that I wanted Randy to use his husbandly authority to try to stop me? But he didn't, knowing that being bossy was a sure way to lose our argument. Instead, he adopted the professorial approach which he successfully used during business negotiations.

"Why accept it when you're already so busy?" he asked.

"I'm not sure. I do feel worn out but am also bored. We've picked up business but it's our usual celebrity security which now interests me as much as watching grass grow. I've been at it for years and need an intellectual challenge like those that you get every day, not the same-old/same-old. These pro bono cases energize me and make me feel whole again," I said.

Randy looked me over.

"Maybe we can work off some of that energy tonight," he said in a serious tone, before grinning.

Chapter 47

Randy didn't take all of my energy but the kids did the following morning. By 10AM I found myself feeling nearly as down as the previous day until my older sister phoned.

Melody was newly married and I asked, "How is married life?"

"It's fun!" she said, exuberantly.

My mood lifted slightly until thinking that it had been a long time since I had fun. Enjoyment and pleasure? Yes. Fun? When had I last had fun?

"It's not Valentine's Day but do you want to hear a supernatural, Valentine's Day story?"

"Of course."

"It'll lift your mood," Melody said.

Apparently I'm not so good at hiding my feelings, I thought.

"Jessica told it to me. She's in my corporate law class."

I waited patiently, having the misfortune of hearing stories from people who enjoy drawing out suspense.

"Jessica is twenty-six, still single after a string of bad relationships. One morning she was bemoaning her fate, vowing to stay in bed all day but forcing herself to go out. Her neighborhood theater was showing Woody Allen's old movie, *Annie Hall*, which she had seen so often that she could repeat some of the dialogue. There was a problem with the heating and she sat shivering until the movie was over, nearly choking on burnt popcorn. She had been invited to a party that night but decided not to go.

"After getting home she told herself that she would always be alone and that the only love she would see would be on a screen. After taking off her makeup and getting into bed, she heard the voice of her deceased grandmother who ordered her to 'dress yourself like the star you are and go to that party!'"

"What did she do?" I asked, unable to contain my curiosity.

"Jessica got dressed, put her makeup back on, and went to the party. It began snowing and she nearly drove off the road and was the last to arrive. Once there, she saw a totally gorgeous guy staring at her. 'My makeup must be ghastly,' she told herself and went to the bathroom to check it. When she returned the man came over and said that he'd seen her in Walmart a week before but was too shy to approach. He asked if she'd noticed him. Not wanting to discourage him, she said she doesn't wear her glasses outside but that if she had seen him she certainly would have remembered him.

"They talked until the party ended and became inseparable. Three months later he proposed on his knee and both cried. 'Every day is a holiday,' she said. Do you feel better now?" Melody asked.

I did.

Chapter 48

Melody's story so cheered me that my mood was lifted when my children streamed into my arms. I was back to normal. "You tend toward depression but snap right back," Randy once told me.

My long-past therapist said the same before explaining depression. "It happens when you're stuck about something, feeling unable to move on so you *depress* your feelings and give up." So what am I stuck about? I asked myself while nuzzling my baby's hair.

This answer came not immediately but an hour later. That apart from my corporate chores which I now did mindlessly, I was challenged by four issues on which movement was going nowhere: Tara's worry about her husband's identity; Asya's sense, which I shared, that the terrifying crime wave was underlain by a sinister plot; Thomas' desire to rescue his daughter, Dakota; and my employee being offered two-hundred-thousand-dollars to murder a Greenwich resident and make it look like an accident. Time to move, I told myself, and picked up the phone.

"Is there any news about our pro bono cases?" I asked Jordan, my assistant.

"Apart from our accountant's blistering e-mail about their cost?" he asked.

"He'll calm down once he sees our quarterly profit. Anything else?"

"I was about to call. Tara's husband, Nick, *does* have an identity problem. We're unable to find anything about him before his marriage when he seems to have popped up from nowhere. Our police contact confirmed his driver's license but this can be gotten with just a birth certificate which is easy to get. We can't find anyone who knew him before he moved to Greenwich and are still looking."

"Huh!" I exclaimed.

"Yes. But Josef's offer of two-hundred-thousand-dollars is from a real person and his background checks out. Clinton is a tech company CEO, his wife's father is president of the company, and their assets are mostly company stock. He comes from Oregon poor and we're checking there too. He has a graduate degree from MIT and the company is fortunate to have hired him according to industry sources. One might even say that his marriage was engineered by the bride's father to gain a gifted CEO."

"He's *that* good," I mused.

"Apparently, he is."

"How is his health? Is he really dying of cancer?" I asked.

"This is where the situation gets tricky," Jordan said.

Chapter 49

"According to workers at his country club, he's in great health if the ability to play tennis is an indicator. Getting his medical record will be tricky."

"But you'll get it," I said.

"We'll get it."

"His marriage is on the rocks," Jordan added.

I said nothing. Jordan is another of those maddening people who enjoy preserving suspense when telling a story.

"She meets her lover on Wednesday mornings at her hairdresser. He sips coffee and watches."

"I wish Randy did that," I mused aloud.

"What?"

"Nothing. Anything else?"

"A startup is eating their business. It's not Clinton's fault but if the company fails, I don't see him staying in Greenwich or the marriage," Jordan said.

"Interesting. Keep looking. Have you discovered any more about Tara's husband?" I asked hopefully.

"One detail. The banking job that he goes to every morning and returns from every evening."

"Yes?"

"He was fired two years ago. I haven't been able to find out why but they may have grown suspicious about his background too," Jordan said.

"That's great work in so little time," I said, knowing that inadequate praise reflects poor management. "We have another pro bono job which make these seem like child's play. A young woman is infatuated with her crooked lover. We're going to break up their romance, pull the stars from her eyes, and bring her home to her waiting father. All without her arrest if she's involved in her boyfriend's larcenies," I said.

"Why are we accepting this impossible task and without payment?" Jordan asked in an exasperated tone.

"Because its success will be great for our business. Dakota's father, Thomas, worked in Washington for decades and knows the important movers-and-shakers," I said.

"Providence is all right if you give it a chance," Jordan said wearily.

"*That's* the attitude!" I said.

But I should have let Jordan have the last word, being unable to improve on it.

Chapter 50

While it isn't in my nature to sit back and wait, our pro bono cases demanded it. Without facts, nothing could be done which might not end up disastrously. "Waiting is always the hardest," Sergeant Alamo of the Greenwich Police Department, a long-time family friend, once said. So I waited.

Meanwhile, like with all mothers, there was much to do. While Asya, our ten-year-old, was privately tutored at home, my toddlers attended a nearby Montessori whose principal was agreeable to having the children's bodyguard close by. This is not an unusual demand in official Washington where a child's bodyguard is often downplayed as being a teaching assistant to inquiring mothers. My toddler's daily absence granted me time to work from my home-office, while caring for my newborn of course.

The Watergate complex proved to be a convivial community, thankfully free from the "how can I use you to get ahead" attitude of hustling Washingtonians. Or maybe it was simply that its afternoon lectures were attended by young mothers and the retired. The talk by newly published author, Kristin Margarita Jorgensen, was exceptionally interesting. Her cynicism about politics gave me ideas to share with my father who was a new United States senator.

Despite her printed conventional biography, a scent of mystery enveloped the author like an intoxicating perfume. The shape of her blue eyes was mournful, almost Eurasian. Her hair was long and gypsy black, and her fashionable long red dress made her seem tall though this was not so. Everything seemed to amuse her as if her vantage point over humanity was Olympian, that she had survived the shocks of an explosive life without being touched by them.

"Washington is America's living theater where the best seats are filled by actors. If every government worker from the President down to the secretaries would operate only two weeks a year, America would be the greatest country in the world."

This statement brought a big laugh and she paused before continuing.

"Some join a political movement because it demands the best in people: courage and self-sacrifice and discipline. Some join because they crave a faith and the movement binds them to a living religion. Some seek power and it promises them a future. Some are idealists and it offers them a crusade. Some hate society and it changes this into a philosophy. Some are lonely and it gives them friends. And some are afraid and it guarantees them victory."

After her talk, I dawdled to be last on line and received a grateful smile upon buying her book. Few authors earn a living wage from their writing, I handed her my impressive business card, having sensed that she would be a valuable hire.

"I would like to discuss a business proposition with you over lunch and will pay you five-hundred-dollars for your time." I said.

Using the successful creative approach that had been made with Josef though certainly not with the five-thousand dollars he was offered. I'm not *that* free with company money.

Chapter 51

Kristin's response was surprise. A free lunch and money were *never* offered to a new author by a grateful reader. She carefully studied my business card before replying.

"Why be so generous?" she asked suspiciously.

"I'm the American manager of a multi-national security company. Hiring talent is my most important duty and I'd like to tell you what we can offer. What do you have to lose?" I asked, with a smile.

While still looking suspicious, perhaps fearing kidnap or worse in crime-filled Washington, I added, "LeDiplomate is open for lunch. If convenient, we can meet there on Thursday at 1:30PM," I said.

LeDiplomate is Washington's equivalent of a Parisian bistro with its shiny red booths, green subway tile, and seafood platters ferried around with grace. Though usually crowded, people didn't yet feel safe after the pandemic ended and business wouldn't be normal. I expected a quiet table to be available on an afternoon.

Margaret in Washington

When Kristin didn't immediately respond, I pressed.

"I have to leave, to feed my newborn and check on my other children. Phone by tomorrow morning if you decide against meeting. I'd be sorry," I said, and left.

I had deliberately spoken of my parenting duties to reassure her, nursing mothers only being considered threatening by uptight men.

The pandemic had increased crime. Being instinctively cautious, I traveled to our meeting with a company bodyguard. To service our Washington business, which had tripled over the previous year, I had hired four retired Washington police officers. One, a rangy, fifty-four-year-old man resembling a younger Clint Eastwood, accompanied me to the restaurant and sat nearby.

Chapter 52

The lunch crowd thinned by the time we arrived, permitting an empty nearby table for my bodyguard who sipped coffee as he peered about the room. Eating would have interfered with his duty. Kristin quickly commented on him.

"That man is watching us," she said.

"He's my bodyguard, a company perk. You're safe so long as you don't make a sudden move," I said with a smile.

"Why do you need for a bodyguard?" Kristin asked.

"It wouldn't say much for our company's protective service if its manager were mugged," I said.

The waiter appeared and I ordered the cheese selection, salmon, and a beet salad. Kristin ordered trout amandine, a mushroom tart, and shrimp salad. We both had ice cream for dessert.

"I couldn't find much online about your company which is unusual nowadays," she said when the waiter left.

"We're an unusual company," I replied.

Then, after pausing to increase her anticipation, I spoke my oft-given spiel.

"My father, in Berlin, is president of the company. He's a former Russian general and our board is made up of retirees from the CIA and Britain's intelligence service. There are two parts to our business. One offers protective services for celebrities and diplomats. The other is paramilitary, doing hostage rescue and other work using former soldiers from Russia, the United Kingdom, and America. We work only for Western governments and you won't find a more ethical outfit," I said.

"Why would you want to hire me?" Kristin asked.

"I liked what I heard during your talk. You're a hard-bitten cynic who has seen everything and lost all illusions. You've seen people under stress and learned the limits of human nature yet manage to keep a vein of idealism too," I said.

"That's is me but what could I do for your company?" Kristin asked.

"We'll talk about that in a while," I said.

Chapter 53

"I've had people check into your background and they've come up with little," I said.

Kristin smiled.

"They've learned that you worked for the government but not where, that you've never been arrested, and that your credit is good. I also know the amounts in your bank and brokerage accounts," I said.

"You shouldn't," Kristin said.

"No, but it's important for us to know. You've probably worked for one of the intelligence services but I won't ask which since you won't tell. What you can is your last salary and why you left," I said.

Kristin chewed on a piece of trout before answering.

"I last earned $120,000 a year, being at the GS-14 rank. I left because I wasn't good enough at the power struggle to advance. I might be too decent, too careful to avoid cruelty or spite, or possibly incite co-workers to be my enemy. Or maybe it's that I'm indifferent to power or it was too hard to be a woman in my setting or all these.

Margaret in Washington

"So I decided to quit and trust to luck. Maybe it's in my character to gamble though not at the racetrack or roulette wheel. More the slot player who stops at a hundred-dollar loss."

Sensing Kristin's honesty, I risked probing further.

"Another personal question: do you have an attachment that would make travel difficult?" I asked.

The arrival of this answer took two bites of trout for her to consider.

"You must already know that I've never been married though not from lack of desire. I'm simply trusting to have the same luck that my older sister had," Kristin said.

Chapter 54

I waited impatiently, sensing that I was about to hear a great story.

"My sister, Ellie, is seven-years older. After a long, disastrous marriage which for some unknown reason she hesitated to leave, she got lucky and her husband left.

"'It's easy to pick out a shiny diamond when you see it in the store but harder to pick it out in the rough,' she said. She'd never lived on her own and when her husband moved out she had to make repairs for the first time. Knowing that the apartment opposite was lived in by a guy and assuming that men always have tools, she knocked on his door to borrow a screwdriver she needed.

"Ellie was thirty-five at the time and the guy looked about twenty, barely out of high school. He turned out to be twenty-nine, an electrical engineer, and much quieter than her ex and the men who usually attracted her. He helped with the repair and left. A few weeks later he asked her out to a show. Afterward, when she invited him in for coffee, he moved close and kissed her. This made her nervous since her husband had left only two months before and she wasn't sure she was ready to date. She *was* lonely but..."

I ignored my food. This was developing into one of those stories that you don't forget.

"She told him her dilemma and he said he understood, which made her decision. As they dated regularly, Ellie became less self-conscious about how young he looked and ignored the advice of friends that she shouldn't get serious about a man soon after separation. She came to believe that what you should seek in a man is the understanding and comfort you get with a good girlfriend, and that it's this which lasts.

"Ellie and Tim married five months ago and she's expecting. She said she feels good all over when she sees him, that they still hold hands in the movies and she doesn't worry when he goes on business trips though he's a hunk. Tim is the kind of diamond that I'm prospecting for," Kristin concluded.

Chapter 55

"Now that you know about me, what's your offer?" Kristin asked.

It was a good question. I slowly chewed a bite of salmon while preparing my reply. How much should I tell her?

"Our company provides more than personal security and para-military services. We also investigate to sort out the puzzles that tear people apart: threats, blackmail, and the like.

"I like your honesty and cynicism and humor. You're someone that I feel we can work with, Spying gives you extraordinary insight into people, the habit of considering their possibilities. Are they this or that and if I can recruit them how can I use them? It's a kind of inside-out thinking that never leaves you," I said.

"I never said I had been a spy," Kristin said.

"No, you didn't but we'll let that matter rest for the moment. Outside novels, in the real world, much of the time, good people do bad things and bad people do good things. This makes moral choices difficult and intelligence count.

"It's a sad fact of life that the people with secrets are likely to be men and that most men don't regard women as their equal. Consequently, they don't trust women or feel comfortable placing their life in the hands of a woman. They would rather hit on a woman, try to get alone with them. The perfect woman case officer is attractive but not sexy, confident without a chip on her shoulder, comfortable about being a woman but not a women's libber.

"Women agents have advantages too. They can control their emotions better than men. They can be braver, more disciplined, and more discreet. They can be invisible whereas a man would immediately be suspect. But they also have one great disadvantage: they must deal with men."

I smiled, took another bite of salmon, and concluded the first part of my pitch.

"Once you've been in the intelligence business it gets under your skin. You're no good for anything else," I said.

Chapter 56

Despite secrecy laws, where a government employee worked isn't hard to learn. Not for certain but hints exist. Was Kristin a case agent? I didn't know. Had she worked for one of the intelligence agencies? Of course.

"Our company was created by military people and follows that practice: that an employee is best either at battle or as a staff worker solving a problem. I've done both but having a family limits me and I need someone to kick around ideas with and occasionally work in the field. Jordan, my assistant, is a West Point graduate and excels in staff work. Our field agents are all men and we lack female talent," I said.

"Are we negotiating?" Kristin asked.

"We're *always* negotiating and my offer will beat anything you'll get elsewhere," I said, with a smile.

I now spoke softly, causing her to lean forward and my words to seem more important.

"Your last salary was $120,000 a year. We will pay you $180,000 plus a bonus based on the company's profit each year. You'll need an appropriate home to host an occasional business party so we'll provide you a house. You'll also get complete medical and dental coverage, a retirement plan in which we'll match every dollar you invest with our two, and one month of vacation a year. There will also be a leased car with your choice of make and color though not a Rolls Royce. A Buick would do fine," I said.

"That's *extraordinary*," Kristin said.

"Not for one of your ability," I said.

A boss can never give too many compliments.

"Where would I be located?" Kristin asked.

"Now in Washington but later in Greenwich, Connecticut where our East Coast office is located and I usually live," I said.

During the silence that followed I sensed Kristin's thoughts. That for a single person, life in a family oriented small town or suburb can be deadly. I was right.

"Your offer is fantastic but can I find my diamond in Greenwich?" she asked.

"Most of our employees are men. You won't be lonely," I said assuredly.

Chapter 57

Kristin accepted my offer despite its lack of a guaranteed lover. I had already made one successful match, between an employee and a newly relocated, lonely scientist, but the stars are not always so aligned. Still, Kristin was an adult, knew the score, and could make her own way.

Our bureaucracy required two weeks for her official hiring so we arranged for her to begin working then. I wanted sooner, needing help with the cases on my plate, but this was not to be. Though having limited authority to hire, the final decision was made by our corporate headquarters in Berlin and this took time. Not that there was much to be done since two of the pro bono cases needed more background information and Dakota's case required finding her. It was with her that I expected Kristin to be most helpful.

Though being the second-oldest child in my family, I had become the sibling that the younger ones came to with their issues, possibly because I was the only one with a family of my own. Melody, my newly married four-year-older sister, attended law school and was considered by the others as a student rather than as head of a household. Thus I came to field many of my younger sisters' dilemmas, those that they felt uneasy about raising with our parents.

These issues weren't about sex. When I asked a psychologist when to have *the* sex talk with my teenage daughters he replied, "Only if you have a question. Teenagers know more about sex than us." He didn't look like he was joking.

Still, I *was* shocked by my sixteen-year-old sister's comment, "I think something is fishy when a girl talks about her amazing sex life since you should spend more time humping than bragging about it. What do you think?"

"Hmm..." I ducked, as my other phone fortunately rang.

Chapter 58

No matter their family bubble, all Americans became affected by the crime wave which infused them with a sense of dread. Having only recently survived the COVID pandemic, our senses became daily hit by news of atrocities: arson attacks on schools causing numerous fatalities; the rape and torture of women in their home and on church premises on two occasions; a grain storage facility being set afire; the sabotage of wireless and electrical and water systems and more.

All lacked a public claim of responsibility unlike the typical terrorist act. They are waiting for something bigger, I thought, mirroring Asya's earlier prediction.

Following the proverb that diligence is the mother of good luck, I called my assistant, Jordan. Though it was early evening when he would be relaxing with his wife and child, my anxiety had overwhelmed good managerial practice.

"Have you learned more about Tara's husband or Josef's proposition?" I asked.

"Tara's husband and the proposition made to Josef," Jordan repeated automatically, before saying, "some."

I waited as he organized his response, being unsure if satisfaction or disappointment awaited me. In the military his orders had been noted for their care, a habit that he continued into the private sector.

"We've gotten initial information though it's hardly explanatory. Nick is not who he says he is and Clinton, who made the two-hundred-thousand-dollar offer to be killed, is still a puzzle.

"Nick arrived in town as a wunderkind, handsome and exuding charm, flush with money and eager to invest, causing few questions. Clinton arrived straight from graduate school with no doubt about his identity. He had manners and looks, was single, and an apparent good marital choice. Which the single daughter of a local tech company owner noticed and acted on."

"Except?" I asked, sensing there was more.

"Except that Clinton has an unusual travel itinerary," Jordan said.

Chapter 59

"Every three months he travels to the small Western town where he grew up," Jordan said.

"What's strange about that. He probably has relatives there and wants to keep up family ties," I said.

"Okay, *except* that he doesn't see them. When I phoned his father, pretending to be an insurance agent with a call concerning his son's policy application, I was told that he hadn't seen him in years. So why does he go back?" Jordan asked.

"To see someone else?" I suggested.

"Right! We dug on the ground, speaking with neighbors, teachers, anyone who might have known Clinton when he was growing up and hit the answer."

I waited impatiently.

"He visits his high school sweetheart with whom he now has two children. They meet at a motel for weekends. His journeys are to maintain contact with his other family. He has no children with his wife," Jordan said.

"What's his financial situation?" I asked.

"That's probably another element since it's not as good as it appears. His wealth comes from his salary and his company isn't doing well. If his shaky marriage falls apart, he'd be left hanging by his father-in-law which isn't an enviable position."

"And the cancer that's supposedly killing him?" I asked.

"We're still checking. It's not easy to get into medical records."

"Okay. You're done extraordinarily well in a short time," I said.

"It smells bad and I distrust his offer to Josef. There's something we're not seeing. Despite what we've learned I feel we're groping and hope for Josef's sake that we don't stumble," Jordan said.

"Trust your instinct," I said, there being no need to say more.

Chapter 60

Only my mother attended my father's swearing-in as a United States senator. Not from lack of pride but because personal security is safest by keeping family details from public knowledge. Some will inevitably leak like the number of a politician's children and their ages. But none of us were permitted to have Facebook accounts and E-mail was restricted to family members, rules that I'll impose on my children too.

After the public ceremony I held a celebratory dinner at my apartment. Here, the talk turned to my dad's latest story which involved a lawyer's self-inflicted wound.

"Personal injury lawyers buy the flashiest, most expensive cars, both from vanity and as advertisement. 'Look how much I made for myself from doing good,' they boast. Thus, just eight-years out of law school, attorney Jones (a pseudonym) was doing well, having won several multi-million-dollar cases with one-third landing in his pocket. Having achieved this though the jurors of the conservative county where he practiced were leery of giving big awards.

"One day, traveling to court in his Maserati, he found himself in the courthouse parking lot with a flock of them. Jurors focus minutely on the lawyers before them, how they dress and particularly what they drive.

"Thereafter, Jones' car became a topic of conversation in the jury room and when jurors deadlocked over how much to award the plaintiff, whether fifty-million-dollars or nothing, the car was discussed and a note was sent to the judge asking how much Jones stood to earn from the award. The plaintiff was awarded seven-million-dollars which, according to Jones, was *much* less than expected. 'My car turned out to be the most expensive Maserati in America,' he told me. Now, Jones drives a Chevy," my dad said.

Chapter 61

After dinner, as my children devoured the sugary treats they weren't allowed at home, I asked my mother, "Where will Claudine go to school?"

Hearing her name, my sixteen-year-old sister's focus turned from her cousins.

"*Where will I go*? Washington schools don't have the greatest academic reputation and not for safety either," she asserted, in a troubled tone.

"Your father and I haven't decided. We're checking private schools," my mother replied firmly.

Claudine visibly relaxed as did I. While all school systems have some good teachers and principals, the reputation of Washington's public schools was dismal.

"I've asked around for nearby schools and two were recommended: Georgetown Day and Sidwell Friends," my dad said.

Claudine didn't look happy. Though an excellent student whose grades were rarely less than an "A," her scrapes were already legendary. Which might have been expected considering what she already survived.

Margaret in Washington

Following several miscarriages and hungering for a larger family, my parents had adopted Claudine. *Rescued* would be a better term since her parents were meth addicts living in a criminal commune far from Greenwich. She had lacked medical and dental care and was removed from her family when a neighbor saw her scrounging for food in their garbage.

Fate or maybe biology had made her a survivor who took guff from no-one. She considers that our best time together is at Greenwich's shooting range, shredding paper targets portraying fiendish men. She's long been an avid reader of *Sherlock Holmes* and wants to work with our company someday.

"You're choosing *my* school?" Claudine asked, with narrowing eyes.

My father, using the guile gained from having parented three older teenagers replied, "Not at all. Both schools give virtual tours. Go online and decide which you'd prefer or find a nearby school that you'd like better."

"More pie anyone?" my mother asked, as all relaxed.

Chapter 62

Claudine's mischievous expression caused me to give her a *watch-it look* she ignored.

"Three friends were talking. One said that after giving birth to her first child, her husband bought her a Jaguar. 'Oh, how sweet,' her friend said. The second woman said that after she gave birth her husband bought her a three-story mansion. 'Oh, how sweet,' the first friend said. The third woman said that after she gave birth her husband sent her to a charm school in Switzerland. 'What did you learn there?' she was asked. 'Now instead of saying, "Kiss my ass," I say, 'Oh, how sweet.'"

Even my very proper mother laughed and my father said with a smile, "I wouldn't want to be the principal of a school that Claudine didn't like."

"No way!" Claudine insisted.

Sensing that something else was bothering her, I later took her aside.

"What's wrong?" I asked.

Taking my hand, Claudine moved me further from the others.

"I may be pregnant," she whispered.

"Are you *sure*?" I whispered.

"My period's late and I've always been regular."

"That's no certain indicator. Did you...?" I asked, being unable to get out the words.

"Once. On maybe not my luckiest day."

"With whom?"

"Garth, in his car at a drive-in, when the theaters were closed during the pandemic. Pretty nineteen-fifties stuff huh?"

"Wherever," I said, dismissively, the circumstance being unimportant.

"I'm glad you felt trusting enough to tell me," I said.

"You were a single mother. I wouldn't feel comfortable telling mom," Claudine said.

"You might be surprised. She's less uptight now than when we were younger."

"It's not that. I'd feel that I'd disappointed her."

"Nothing you ever do would cause her to feel that. We consider you a wonder and love you to death," I said.

"Especially considering where I started out," she said, referring to her meth-addicted parents.

I took charge.

"Have you tested yourself?" I asked.

"No."

"That's first. Your worry may turn out to be only a painful lesson," I said.

"To stay out of boy's cars," Claudine said.

"And if not, to keep your panties on," I said, sweetly.

Chapter 63

"You look angry. Is it me?" Claudine asked.

"Did Garth force himself on you?" I asked, with clenched teeth.

Claudine stared at me before answering.

"No, he's shy. It was more like me forcing myself on him. I'd brought condoms and was ready. Why are you so angry?" she asked.

"Because of what you survived as a child. Scrounging for food like a mouse and the rest. My childhood was very different but, both being adoptees, I always felt protective of you. If Garth had hurt you..." I said, becoming silent as rage swept through me.

"Nothing bad happened," Claudine said, reassuringly, and touched my arm.

"What do you know about pregnancy tests?" I asked, as my Big Sister role took over.

"Nothing," said Claudine.

"Okay, I'll tell you what I once had to learn. At-home pregnancy tests use the human chorionic gonadotropin (hCG) hormone to detect pregnancy and some tests are more sensitive to it than others. This is why some tests work earlier when you have less of the hormone and others won't show up positive until later when you have a higher amount.

"When an egg is fertilized, your body begins producing hCG. During early pregnancy, hCG levels double every two to three days, peaking by the end of your first trimester. Pregnancy tests look for how much hCG is present in your urine.

"A home pregnancy test is more accurate the longer you wait to take it. Testing on the day of your expected period or after yields a more conclusive answer. If you test too early you could get a false negative and have to test again later. Ready to shop?"

Claudine nodded and, as we grabbed our coats, made her second stunning statement that day.

"You know how I've always said that I want to be a detective."

"You read *Sherlock Holmes* in grade school," I said.

"Yes. Well now I'm thinking that I might want to become a doctor."

Chapter 64

Drugstores have nearly as many brands of pregnancy tests as candy bars, I thought, as we stood before the shelf, Claudine stared at her Big Sister and waited.

"I used the First Response Early Result test. It's reportedly the most sensitive and gives an accurate result up to five days before your period. The stick's curvy handle makes it easy to hold as you pee on it. Do you want the digital version that uses words instead of lines to report your result?" I asked.

"*Dope!*" she responded, with a grin,

Being cued into teenage slang, I correctly interpreted this word to mean *awesome* and bought the kit.

"Why does this one cost so much more?" she asked, reaching for the Natalist Test Pack.

We read the label. Though costing four-times as much, this kit could be used for up to five days before your period and professed to be ninety-nine-percent accurate. It came with ovulation tests that measure the level of the luteinizing hormone which increases just before ovulation. A positive result means ovulation is likely within the next twenty-four or forty-eight hours.

"There are seven ovulation tests and four pregnancy tests in each box. I don't expect to make a habit of this," Claudine said, replacing it on the shelf.

It took willpower for me not to say, "I should hope not!" Having been glad that I didn't after identifying the anxiety which lay beneath Claudine's smile. She was as terrified as I had been and every woman is when facing the possibility of an unplanned pregnancy.

"Let's go to your apartment," Claudine said, wanting to avoid the possibility of questions from our mother.

There, after reading the instructions together, she tested herself while I prepared dinner. Ten minutes later she sidled beside me.

"It was negative. I'll use the second test tomorrow," she whispered.

As we hugged, I egotistically thought that I couldn't take another stress just then.

Chapter 65

There can be a turning point in a person's life, a sudden shifting of events and movements as during a battle. It may not only be a milestone, a numerically fixed place, but can occur in a person's mind, indicating a change of direction with consequences that are recognized only much later. It may be foreseeable but not with certainty. My turning point came right after Claudine's worry ended.

She was certainly not pregnant, having used both tests in the package and both results were negative.

"I've learned from this experience," Claudine said.

"What did you learn?" I asked.

"That trust is better than love. Love is unpredictable and hurts but trust is dependable and reliable."

"Which is the kind of boy you want," I said.

"*No cap*," she said.

Though understanding this teenage lingo to mean, *that's true*, I made a

145

disapproving face, being both A Mother as well as A Big Sister.

"You're perkier," Randy observed that night.

"I had good news today. It lowered the stress in my life," I said.

"What was that?"

I felt free to answer since Randy doesn't gossip.

"Claudine worried that she was pregnant and she isn't," I said.

This startled him even more than it had me.

"I still think of her as a child," Randy said.

"Considering what she endured before entering our family, she'll never be a little girl. Now she wants to be a doctor," I said.

"She's always talked of becoming a detective so that's an improvement," Randy said.

I said nothing but gave him a *look*. Because of its potential danger, Randy doesn't consider my work fit for a woman. His heart holds his teenage image of a Navy Seal. A male sailor of course.

Chapter 66

My mood didn't lower even after hearing my dad's depressing news.

"Asya is one smart girl," he said.

I waited, expecting more.

"The FBI now believes that the crime wave is more than just that, that something bigger is coming," he said.

"That was Asya's prediction a month ago," I said.

My father nodded.

"Do they sense what it might be?" I asked.

"No, but the Homeland Security Advisory Level has been raised from yellow to red, its highest. Maybe the kids should be kept home for a while," he said.

"Maybe. How do you like the life of a senator?" I asked, changing to a happier subject.

My father thought silently for a minute.

"The best part of my day, apart from when I'm with our family of course, is my morning walk. Breathing in calm from the flower beds while cars inch along clogged roads."

"You have a security guard with you?" I asked, hoping for an affirmative answer.

"Two. The government is being cautious," he said.

"That's good but I'd feel better if you admired the flowers from within my armored SUV," I said.

Ignoring this suggestion, my father continued.

"My schedule yanks me between the Hart and Dirksen buildings with reporters seeking on-the-spot interviews. Most work is done between Tuesdays and Thursdays in committee hearings, floor votes, working lunches, constituent meetings, and public appearances. When in my office suite I'm often engaged with one set of visitors in a conference room while another waits across the hall. I'm briefed before each meeting and try to remember faces for the future.

"Days are tiring with staff members lined outside my door, each needing an answer that a senior staffer can't give. I must also approve all press releases and statements and make phone calls."

"You need a hideaway," I said, overwhelmed by the demands of his position.

"Oh, all senators have one: a semi-secret second office tucked in a nook of the vast Capital."

Chapter 67

Only after speaking with my father did I realize what had been depressing me: that I was focusing on my business problems as stumbling blocks rather than as opportunities from which the working through would grant satisfaction. Sitting at my desk, I briefly wrote each task and what needed doing: Tara's husband, Nick, must be accurately identified after which she need decide what to do; the real motive for Clinton's puzzling offer of two-hundred-thousand dollars for his murder must be learned; and how to wean Dakota from her criminal boyfriend.

Feeling back in control, I phoned my assistant, Jordan, seeking skeptical analysis from one of different experiences than me. I didn't get a chance before he joyously proclaimed, paraphrasing the old AOL line, "We've got news! Which case do you want to hear about first?"

"Who is Nick?" I asked.

"*That's* a story. Do you remember Chicago's twenty-nine-million-dollar armored car robbery four years ago?"

"Vaguely. Didn't the robbers get away?" I asked.

"Not quite. The gang consisted of three brothers and a fourth man, a childhood friend who shot them and fled with the loot. He was identified by a robber on his deathbed but was never found. The brothers were mob connected and the surviving robber is being sought both by them and the FBI."

"Nick is that man," I interrupted.

"He is, and Tara's anger is the least of his problems. Once caught, he wouldn't be safe in any jail, and Tara needn't bother about getting a divorce since he's still married to another woman."

"That leaves her with two problems," I said.

"What are they?"

"Remaking her life and keeping safe from gangsters who think that she knows where the stolen money is," I said.

"What's her best option?"

"Maybe like Nick, to try to disappear," I said, after a thoughtful silence.

Chapter 68

"Claudine called me for advice," Jordan said.

Though our families had become close, this reaching out surprised me. Why had she asked *him* for guidance rather than *me*? The explanation followed.

"She thought that I'd be more expert about this matter than you."

"Huh!" I said, having never rid myself of this immature expression.

"She wanted to know how effective it is to kick a threatening guy in the balls," Jordan said.

Claudine's interest didn't surprise me. Before her adoption by my parents, she lived with crazed, meth-addled parents and their criminal pals. Her attitude had inevitably become to hit first and, if needed, to hit again and apologize later if you made a mistake. Her world view was to take care of yourself, your family, and your friends, a notion that I shared.

"What did you tell her?" I asked, with interest.

"I said that boys have been accidentally hit in the groin since childhood so have quick reflexes to avoid it. That kicking a guy there from behind may momentarily stun him but also makes you too easy to grab. That you should go for his eyes if you're close or punch him in the nose while holding a roll of quarters," Jordan said.

"That's good advice. Did she ask anything else?"

"Yes, what to do if he has a knife," Jordan said.

"Then you run!" I said.

"That's what I told her," Jordan said.

"I'd kill anyone who hurt her," I said, after a pause.

"A Momma Bear protects her tribe. I heard stories about you in Berlin from the head of the BND (*Bundesnachrichtendienst*, Germany's Federal Intelligence Service). She said that you have a 'take no prisoner attitude' but are thoughtful, that you don't just smash people."

"Never give an enemy a second chance. If you mess with someone, you have no right to complain when they return the favor," I said.

Chapter 69

"So, what do we do about Tara?" Jordan asked.

"Her case is pro bono, a work from the heart. She worried about her husband's identity and you discovered it. Tell her what we learned, that our job is over, and suggest that she search her house for the stolen funds. If the money is there, we could educate her now to establish a new identity far away," I said.

"Does the company do that too?" Jordan asked.

"When it's needed by good people," I said.

Then, changing the conversation, I asked, "Have you learned more about Josef's problem?"

"Yes. Things have developed there too. Clinton grew up in a small Oregon town which he visits every two months. Since he flies a lot on company business this aroused no notice. According to his golfing buddies, he has no contact with his family, being estranged from them since graduate school.

"I checked this by calling his father, pretending to be an insurance agent who was investigating Clinton before issuing a policy and found some puzzling facts. He isn't alienated from his family though not seeing them often. His father knows of Clinton's marriage and business success and believes these keep him from visiting since his lower-class origin doesn't fit with his current lifestyle. So the next question is that if he's not visiting his family, why does he travel to that town every two months?"

"You learned a lot," I said.

"His father is a Vietnam vet and we became friendly talking about military life. But I've gotten all that I can over the phone. For more, I'll have to go out there."

"Okay. Vacation there for a week with your family and bill the company," I said.

"It's alright to take them?" he asked, with surprise.

"It is if I say so. You're not working for the government anymore," I said.

Chapter 70

Three has long seemed a magic number so I wasn't surprised when my third problem phoned.

"When should I expect my daughter?" Thomas asked.

His casual tone implied this was a small, easily accomplished undertaking but bringing an errant adult home from her beloved criminal housemate is not a task for the faint hearted. Yet, my annoyance wasn't caused by this but because in the turmoil of Claudine's distress I had forgotten this job. Which is something that a good manager should not do.

"I'm working on it. I have another call and will get back to you," I said, in a rushed but confident tone.

The vacation days that my new agent, Kristin, negotiated before starting weren't yet over but I phoned her anyway. Dealing with sudden crises is a way of life in the security business and one that she would have to adjust to.

"I know I promised you a few more days but we have a situation that needs you," I said.

"Sure. I was starting to get bored," Kristin said, readily.

"Can we meet at my apartment in an hour?" I asked.

"Be there."

I gave her my address and, while waiting, straightened my home-office/bedroom from the damage of my toddlers.

Kristin arrived promptly and I filled her in.

"Dakota is our client's twenty-four-year-old daughter. She's living with her meth-selling boyfriend who she met in college before he entered his current business with chums more unsavory than him. She's cut off contact with her father because he disapproves of her lifestyle and he wants her back," I said.

"You're seeking a miracle," Kristin said.

"A small one."

"What are your company's Rules of Engagement?" Kristin asked.

"We have only two: do what it takes to succeed, and don't get caught," I said.

"This sounds like fun," Kristin said, with a smile.

Margaret in Washington

"I sensed you were the woman for the job," I said, returning her smile.

Chapter 71

I was pleased by Kristin's friendly impenetrable smile and gracious manner. Detecting that her high ideals and intelligence had not frozen into inflexibility and self-righteousness, that she enjoyed people but could remain detached and crafty. This endowed her with evasive morals and the capacity to regard another as expendable. Though appearing soft and complaisant, she was hard inside, making her a perfect agent.

Being single, without a private commitment, freed her for idealism and cynicism but also meant a private sadness. Condemning her to the depression from which she recoiled in others but accepted in herself.

She was a compassionate woman but without illusions. One who had been close enough to death to understand the frailty of human striving but would remain loyal to doing her best in the sight of God.

"Who is *she*?" my toddler, Donna, asked, upon bursting into the room, having geared up for a world class tantrum until seeing the visitor.

"She's mommy's friend. We work together," I said.

Donna peered pensively at Kristin before asking, "Do you have a gun too?"

Though obviously surprised by the question, Kristin responded quickly.

"Yes, but my gun is at home."

Then, after picking up a toy, Donna left the room.

"My Greenwich home has security rooms. Guns are visible during drills and carried by our bodyguards," I said, feeling that Kristin should be given an explanation lest she consider me crazed.

"I didn't doubt you were a good mother," she said, sensing my concern.

"More apple cake?" I asked, before returning the conversation to Dakota's rescue.

Chapter 72

"We've found where she and Snake are living," I said.

"Snake?" Kristin interrupted.

"Yes. You'd hope that Dakota would at least have chosen a lover with a regular name but that's what he's known by. We're not sure where he is but she lives in a St. Louis high-rise. A party building with a pool, in a good part of town and quite nice according to the report. You could move in and meet people by hanging around the pool and exercise center."

"It's a plan but not how to separate them. Judgment tends to flee when love walks in and you said Dakota loves him," Kristin said.

"I thought how we might deal with that too," I said.

A smile flit across Kristin's face. We were on the same page.

"The way to break them apart is to change her view of him from that of sexy, hustling renegade to being vile and a serial cheater," I said.

"This sounds interesting," Kristin said.

"We're going to send her faked photos of Snake having sex with children and teenagers. He won't get to talk his way out since he'll be jailed because of alleged involvement in a sex trafficking ring. During these events her father will show up to offer sympathy and hopefully bring her home," I said.

Kristin finished a bite of apple cake before speaking.

"I hope you never get mad at me," she said.

"You needn't worry. That would be personal. This is business," I said.

Chapter 73

Kristin's hippie dress had small flowers and a low neckline. Not posh Washington style but good for her upcoming job. Noting my interest, she explained.

"When working, I wore a uniform that could fit into many social slots. Cream-colored silk or white cotton blouses with black slacks, expensive black boots, and a linen or light woolen jacket depending on the season.

"I'd carry a Hermes silk scarf and gold earrings in a buttoned inside pocket. When just hanging out I'd dump the jacket in the car and roll up the sleeves on the blouse. By wearing the coat I could look casual business and working. With the scarf and earrings I could pass anywhere short of a formal affair where I'd seem a caterer.

"I might need any of these looks while doing reconnaissance, especially if the scene involved security people who are allergic to publicity."

"You'll have whatever you need. Our company doesn't stint on expenses or support. I'll send along two on-call heavies to hang-out nearby. We've never lost an agent," I said, supportively. "

"Airline travel won't work with a weapon so we'll arrange for local delivery. Do you have a preference?" I asked.

"Nothing exotic, a small 9MM," Kristin said.

From a locked desk drawer, I retrieved three pistols.

"They're all 9MM and hold six rounds. The Kimber is the smallest, with smooth edges for concealed carry. The Sig Sauer has large sights and is easy to shoot and control. These are single action. The Springfield Armory holds eight rounds and can be fired single or double action. Which would you like?" I asked.

"I like small but double-action is safer. I'd prefer the Springfield," Kristin said.

"It'll wait for you in St. Louis. Do you want a switchblade too?" I asked, taking it from the drawer.

Kristin fingered it, opening and closing the blade.

"One shouldn't take a knife to a gunfight," she said, with a smile.

"No, but they do have uses," I said, not smiling.

Chapter 74

Another person to worry about, I selfishly thought, after Kristin left. Managing a security company is more like being a military commander than a civilian administrator. If a store or typical company makes a mistake, a sale might be lost or a company go broke. If our employee made a mistake, they could be injured or killed, as might the person they were protecting.

Because worry distorts behavior, I try to minimize it and thus welcomed my toddler son's arrival. Guessing that he intended to complain about his sister, as she might have earlier meant to complain about him, but I was wrong.

"There's a monster under my bed," he whispered earnestly, as if the creature were eavesdropping.

"A young child's reality only occasionally intersects with an adult's. Telling them that their view of the world isn't accurate won't work," his pediatrician once told me.

"Hmm..." I murmured, embracing James tightly.

"It says nasty things," he said.

"What does it say?" I asked, making a horrified face.

James calmed, having gained a grown-up ally in the war with his tormentor.

"It says I'm no good and it's going to eat me," he said, in a trembling voice.

"That's *never* going to happen. Not so long as you have a ray gun," I said firmly.

"A *gun*?" he said, hopefully.

A firm rule in our gun-owning household is that children *never* touch them.

"A special gun, a monster-killing gun. We'll buy it today so you'll be ready. After tonight, there'll be no more monsters. Not ever!"

I saw the hint of a smile on James' face as I Googled for the address of the nearest toy store.

Chapter 75

I discovered that my promise to James couldn't be easily kept. Had I unlawfully wanted to buy him a real gun this wouldn't have been hard. But the safe toy gun that he needed had become politically incorrect.

Decades ago when Western movies were popular, Wild West cap guns, toy Dick Tracy handguns and toy space guns were widely available but not now. What James required, a noisy battery-powered, flashing-light plaything, could only be purchased online.

Some of these toys closely resembled genuine guns and were dangerous, like the realistic AK-47 assault rifle and replica Luger. Nor would I buy a toy gun that released anything but water, having no faith that a pellet would not find its mark in a person. My advice to mothers about such a gift is brief: lose it or break it.

What satisfied James was a vintage 1980s, Radio Shack Galactic Space Pistol with red-and-green pulsating lights. This was definitely the correct choice since its professed use is "to defend your territory against the aliens."

Margaret in Washington

His twin, Donna, joined us as we shopped and insisted on one too. Thus for eighty dollars, which included free shipping, both children now felt protected from peril. But did Kristin feel safe too, I wondered, as her situation re-entered my thinking.

Chapter 76

My business agony was immediately swapped by a forlorn call from a college chum, Jane Ellen. Our lives had drastically changed since those days, mine into work and motherhood and hers into serial dating and career. We each envied the other, she for my marriage and children and I for her college degree. I dropped out of college after becoming pregnant and my graduation, through online study, might occur when my toddlers graduated grade school if ever.

While having a degree wouldn't affect my career advancement or relationship with my doctorate-holding husband, it might color my children's future plans when they were older. Maybe.

"I got a call from Samantha this morning," she began.

Samantha was another college chum.

"Yes," I said.

This sounded like the beginning of a long conversation and I rubbed James' back to keep him still. Kids are sometimes like kittens.

"You remember, she was the loser of us three," Jane Ellen said.

"Uh huh," I murmured, being unsure of the expected response.

"Our assignments were in on time and hers were always late. We got A's and her C's were gifts from teachers pushing for sainthood. After graduating with a biology degree, she became a part-time grounds keeper while figuring herself out."

"Uh huh," I agreed, still trying to figure out where this was going.

"I made *ten times* what she did and dated guys who made even more but she's married and pregnant and look at me," Jane Ellen said.

I remained briefly silent. No reassuring comment had entered my mind.

"What's her husband like?" I finally asked.

"He's an auto mechanic. 'A smart, hard-working guy,' she said but still I probably make *ten times* more."

Sensing James' impatience, I said, "You're smart and beautiful. Your time will come."

But will it if she remains so choosy? I mused.

Chapter 77

Helping others with ordinary difficulties like Jane Ellen's enabled me to tolerate the critical work situations for which I was responsible. They were smaller, contained, and resolvable. If not, they were for Heaven and fate to settle and out of my league.

As days passed without word from Kristin, I second-guessed myself. She was a good hire but had it been correct to send her in harms way. She might have been an intelligence analyst, not an operative, and smart can't always substitute for quick. Still, Napoleon said that his best generals were the lucky ones and I had sensed she was that.

This worry ended a week later when I heard from Otto, one of the two heavies that I had sent to accompany Kristin in her search for Dakota.

"Why are *you* calling?" I asked abruptly.

"Kristin is sedated, in the hospital," he said.

Sedated? Hospital? Regaining control, I asked in a matter-of-fact tone, "What happened?"

"Oh, she'll be fine. She was nauseous with a worsening pain in her stomach. We rushed her to the hospital and a laparoscopic cholecystectomy was done."

"What's that?" I asked quickly.

"Not as bad as it sounds. It's a minimally invasive procedure, using a camera and surgical tool to remove a gallstone. She'll be fine. The only follow-up advice given was to eat a Mediterranean diet and no fast-food."

"Where do things stand with Dakota's rescue?" I asked.

"*That*'s a story. She's in another wing of the hospital. Kristin will visit her soon," Otto said.

Chapter 78

Though expecting to hear of a disaster, I said calmly, "Tell me from the beginning."

Otto's speech lost its excitement as he spoke.

"We arrived in St. Louis to find Dakota gone and not knowing where her boyfriend, Snake, lived. We eventually found him in a building housing a bar with an apartment above. After surveilling for a day and a night and getting nowhere, Kristin dressed like a hooker and went in."

"You let her go in alone?" I asked.

My mothering instinct had briefly flared. Kristin was an adult, could assess risk, and I had certainly gone alone into risky situations.

"It seemed a gamble worth taking," Otto said.

"Yes," I agreed, and he continued.

"She ingratiated herself with hangers-on for several nights and things seemed to be going fine until they didn't. One night when the bar closed, we saw everyone leave except her. We waited twenty-minutes, picked the lock on the door at the rear of the building, and followed the noise to the upstairs apartment. There, we found Kristin being held prisoner by Snake and a man claiming to be a lawyer. Snake just grinned when we asked for Dakota's location."

Otto paused and I heard a voice in the background. "Be there in a minute," he called out.

"Kristin's surgery is over. She's fine, in the Recovery Room. Kristin ordered us to tape the men to chairs facing away from each other. She said that if Snake would provide no useful information that he was of no value to them and hadn't been of value to society for some time, a situation which she intended to remedy. If he didn't reveal Dakota's location, she would shoot him with no more concern than she would for a rabid dog and do the same for his lawyer. 'America has too many lawyers,' she said casually.

"The lawyer said, 'You can't kill us. The police don't kill,' and Kristin replied, 'That's true but we're not police. I'll count to three,' and she slowly did. At two, the lawyer screamed, 'Tell them!' which Snake ignored.

"Before firing at the lawyer, Kristin held her finger to her lips to indicate he should play dead. He did and as the gunshot receded from our ears, Kristin turned toward Snake and said, 'The lawyer's dead. Now your count begins. At 'two' Snake told us where Dakota was."

Chapter 79

"Is Kristin Russian?" Otto asked.

"She has a Russian grandfather who was in the military. Why do you ask?"

Not being surprised since Kristin's behavior demonstrated foreign experience. She couldn't have been simply a desk-bound analyst, I thought.

"I sensed it," Otto said. "Her action reminded me of what happened in Syria forty years ago when terrorists attacked foreigners with kidnappings and truck bombs. When two-hundred Marines were killed in Beirut in one bombing, America did nothing despite having good evidence that the act was planned in Iran. Reagan was advised to blast Syria's Iranian embassy with a Cruise missile but refused, feeling that the evidence wasn't *certain*. Russia wasn't so cautious.

"When five of their diplomats were kidnapped for ransom, *Spetsnaz* (Russian Special Forces, a contraction of *spetsial'noe naznacheniya,* "of special purpose") were sent to the villages where the kidnappers originated. The towns were sacked and bodies were mutilated. One of the kidnapped Russians died but the others were released and no Russian was ever kidnapped again."

Kristin did well but I couldn't help worrying about her mindset. People tend to view morality in Biblical terms and violating these norms can mark one, even if the action would find favor with Heaven.

"How is Dakota?" I asked.

"Not so good. She was gang-raped and beaten but the physical bruises are minor. She'll need psychotherapy but you can assure her father that her attraction to men like Snake is gone."

"Let's hope," I said.

I felt relieved. Two jobs down, one to go.

"There's one more thing," Otto said.

"What's that?" I asked.

"The lawyer who Kristin threatened says that he has vital information but will only give it to her boss. She really scared him."

Chapter 80

I wondered what the lawyer's "vital information" could be. Certainly not of a local crime or typical one. The current widespread crimes had been far from that: the arson of government buildings and crop storage facilities; the murder of police officers; the bombing of inhabited schools; the rape and murder of women in churches. It was as if serial mad men traveled American highways. Or was ten-year-old Asya's suspicion correct: that these heinous acts were the cover for an upcoming far greater evil.

"Set up an audio-video meeting for me with the man. Don't give him my name and I'll conceal my identity," I said.

"Okay. I'll get back to you," Otto said.

I felt uneasy after hanging up. Though my instincts are good, they're not perfect. I wanted another person's opinion of the lawyer since what he said might force me to act. But was he volunteering information to protect himself or because it was so horrendous that it pushed him onto the side of the right and good?

I phoned my father. Though now a United States senator, he had long been an esteemed attorney. Who could better judge another lawyer's validity?

"Dad, I need an important favor," I said.

"If it's within my power," he said, as I expected.

"Briefly, we've just rescued a young woman from a criminal and his lawyer will volunteer *vital information* but only to me. I must judge if it's of national importance or is worthless.

"He's in St. Louis and our conversation will be via audio-video. I'd like you to listen in and assess his truthfulness. As a fellow lawyer, your instinct would be far better than mine," I said.

"It sounds fascinating and better than reading the paperwork covering my desk. Just tell me when," he said.

Chapter 81

"He's scared, having gotten into matters above his head," Otto said, when we spoke two days later.

"Things didn't match courtroom decorum," I agreed.

"No. He was eager to meet though the setting he chose is weird even for me," Otto said.

I waited silently, as he paused.

"It was in the back of a club that is popular with millennials though I can't imagine why: *Club Sing Sing.*"

"Huh?" I gasped, involuntarily.

"That was my reaction when he told me. Entrance into the club is gained by telling a password, *Capone,* or of another 1930s gangster, to a bruiser in a prison guard uniform. Waiters wear orange prison garb with a numberson its back. Inside looks ordinary enough except that on a small stage covered by a curtain is a historic electric chair that had been used to execute criminals."

Otto paused again as I remained speechless.

"Each diner's ticket has a number on its back. The tickets are placed in a bucket and one is picked at 10:00PM. The winner volunteers for their mock execution with the audience applauding a good performance and the condemned 's table charge being waived."

"A strip show would be less depraved," I said.

"I agree. For whatever reason the attorney felt safe here though he was jumpy enough," Otto said.

"You told him of the audio-video arrangement at 8:00PM tomorrow?" I asked.

"That was what you wanted and he agreed," Otto said.

"Anything else?" I asked.

"His final words: that while he wasn't always honest, he does have standards and is patriotic. That even the gang wouldn't touch this job and someone must stop it."

Chapter 82

Though being computer literate, the online setup was beyond my capability but certainly not my husband's. Randy has a doctorate in computer science and I rely on him for technology issues. Moreover, I know that all he learns remains confidential so I had him listen in on our meeting in case a problem developed though none did.

With my veil-covered face and using voice-altering software, I didn't fear being identified. The video connection was so good that I saw beads of sweat on the lawyer's face as he spoke in a trembling voice.

"I want your guarantee of safety," he said.

"You have it. Our goal was Dakota's rescue. We recognize that your role was as an intermediary and have no quarrel with you," I said.

My not quite true concession moved the conversation along as he sighed and visibly relaxed.

"Yes. I'm a patriot and won't do some things no matter how much money is offered."

"You'd best tell me what's involved," I said, evenly.

Though being alone, he looked around to confirm that nobody was in the room. He lit and drew heavily on a cigarette before speaking.

"You know of the recent crime wave: rapes, murders, school burnings."

"Yes," I said.

"It's unsettled everybody. Created an atmosphere of terror, a feeling of instability and fear of what'll happen next."

"The purpose of terror is to create a feeling of helplessness," I said.

"Yes, but that's not its ultimate purpose here."

"Which is?" I asked, hoping to speed the conversation alone.

"To decapitate America's military, render it helpless in one fell swoop but apparently as a criminal and not a terrorist act," he said.

As we spoke I had occasionally glanced at my father's face on part of my monitor. His even, judicious expression was now gone.

Chapter 83

The silence lengthened as I considered my next question. His response stunned me. I had been prepared to learn of a drug deal or robbery but not this. I suddenly felt as I had two years before where, in Moscow, the peace of the world crumbled as a dangerous plot unfolded.

"How exactly do they plan to do this?" I asked, calmly.

"I don't know. The gang hasn't yet learned and are uneasy because of the risk. You can get away with selling meth but kill government officials and you'll be hunted to the ends of the earth."

My father texted me, "Ask who offered this job to the gang," and I did.

"A teniente of the Sinaloa Cartel."

"What is a *teniente*?" I asked.

"A lieutenant, the second highest position in a drug cartel. They supervise the hitmen and *falcons,* street level watchers reporting on police and rival group activities. A teniente can usually carry out only low-profile murders without their boss' permission. The pandemic wrecked this business model, causing members to seek new work without approval from their boss which is risky."

"With Snake in jail, who in his gang would know the identity of this teniente?" I asked.

"Boots is the real boss. Snake was low-level, tolerated because he could be funny and was liked."

"Why is he called Boots?" I asked.

"That's from his high-school days. He nearly kicked a school-mate to death for making a crack about his height. He's sensitive about being short and wears elevator shoes."

"What's your relationship with the gang now that Snake's been arrested?" I asked.

"Snake kept his mouth shut and they still use me. It wouldn't be healthy for me were he to talk or they learn of our meeting."

More questions? I texted my father and he replied *no*.

"You're no longer in danger from us. We will hire your services for a seventy-five-hundred-dollar per month retainer. This is for all your services that we require but your time commitment will likely be small," I told the attorney.

"That is most generous," he said, knowing that it wouldn't be healthy to reject my offer.

"Give Otto your bank's wiring instructions for payment. I'll be in touch," I said, and ended the connection.

I phoned my father.

"What did you make of him?" I asked.

"Sleazy but truthful so long as he's afraid."

"I plan to keep him that way," I said.

Chapter 84

Even a mother needs a parent sometimes and I needed one then. Feeling exhausted after speaking with the lawyer, I told myself that I was juggling too many things. My father agreed though his life was equally harried. But, as I had already learned, a parent's life-long task is to make things easier for their children and my dad now did.

"Do nothing until you hear from me. I'll contact an FBI official I know and he'll likely take it from here," he said.

I couldn't argue since it was now my baby's breastfeeding time. But even then I couldn't avoid a parenting problem, though it was now that of a friend.

Mothers need support from other mothers, who sometimes seem the only ones to completely understand them. Though not being a new mother, I had joined their group after learning about it from a posting in my apartment building's foyer. A chatty phone call and invitation to attend it followed.

Brenda was the mother of a seven-week-old, struggling as a single parent after her boyfriend left. She was thoughtful and a bit of a philosopher as I quickly learned.

"Our pursuit of love is a foolish dream if we hope to harvest its beauty without the pain of its expression. But love's pain has the good of forcing us to move into something greater than ourselves and ideas.

"I loved being partnered with Lloyd but knew he wasn't everything. Now, as a single mother, I've gained a strength and identity that I never would have gotten were I still partnered. I've learned to create a community with people that I trust and who love my child. I no longer fear parenting alone if I must."

I felt calmer after Brenda spoke. Life is with people and you have many good ones supporting you, I told myself.

Chapter 85

My calm didn't last. Two days later I received a hand-delivered letter which demanded attention. The Director of the FBI requested my help "on a matter of national security."

While my dad's contact was obviously good, I doubted that my father had wanted my continued involvement. Yet you *are* involved, I told myself, even if my only goal had been to bring Dakota home.

My invitation might not have come so quickly had not the latest crime, a kidnapping, rocked the nation and been within the FBI's historic jurisdiction. Its victim, Stephanie, the fourteen-year-old daughter of the mayor of St. Louis, was grabbed while on a sleep-over with a girlfriend, Louisa, who provided details.

She and Stephanie were trying on makeup when the kidnapper appeared in the doorway. Threatening them with a gun, he warned them to keep silent as he gagged and bound the friend's arms and legs before gagging Stephanie and binding only her arms. The kidnapper then cut all the clothes from Louisa, as an apparent message to Stephanie's parents, before leaving with her through the house's unlocked side door.

Stephanie's parents had been at a fundraiser that evening, leaving the girls in the care of an elderly housekeeper who went to bed early. Only after the parents returned home and glanced into their daughter's room did they discover what happened.

The authorities wanted to keep the abduction quiet until hearing from the kidnapper but Louisa's presence made this impossible. While awaiting the kidnapper's demand, they hesitated to speak the truth which all knew: that Stephanie's survival became less likely with every hour of captivity.

Chapter 86

A boss must often make a painful decision like whether to fire an employee or order their unwanted assignment. Kristin deserved a rest, as did Stephanie though their situations couldn't be compared.

Would I have made the same decision had I not received the FBI director's letter? Probably not since Dakota's rescue was a private matter and crime is the government's purview. But I could not refuse his plea, nor did Kristin.

"I hoped for time off to recover," she said, as we were being driven to our meeting with the FBI director.

"Which you would have if it weren't for this. When it's over, I don't want to see or Otto for a while. The two of you can check out Montreal on company's expense," I said.

"You *are* informed," Kristin said, with a faint blush.

"That's my job," I said.

The FBI building is an intimidating, buff-colored, low-rise concrete structure with windows of bronze-tinted glass. Its no-nonsense architecture is fit for a national police headquarters or movie set with its government-drab, factory-like interior of hard floors, harsh light, and long corridors.

We were met at the door by a svelte, thirtyish woman in a gray business suit. After receiving visitor credentials, we followed her to an office containing deep carpet and aged wood furniture. The ruddy-cheeked, white mustached, sixtieth man who greeted us had the look of a retired Chairman of the Board but his eyes were sharp and alive.

"I'm pleased that you agreed to help us," he said, extending his hand.

"I didn't feel we had a choice," I said."

"Fate sometimes places us in such position," he said, with an understanding smile.

We smiled too and then got down to business.

Chapter 87

Though not expecting an intimate meeting, the room quickly became packed. Few bureaucrats would avoid the career boost of a meeting with their agency's director. Nor did the meeting's format surprise me.

Each participant described Stephanie's kidnapping and their follow-up activity. My face reflected rapt attention as my mind wandered. Awful as this crime was, it had followed others and was merely a prelude to the main event: the killing of American's military leaders.

Though knowing this, the Director listened with equally apparent interest to the reports from fingerprint and DNA analyses, and the statements of neighbors. Missing was a viable plan.

Finally, he faced us.

"What is your assessment?"

Kristin turned toward me and I cleared my throat.

"Stephanie's kidnapping and the other crimes, each more awful than the last, seem more designed to spread confusion and terror, to fog minds as prelude to a mammoth event similar to the 9/11 terror attacks. But one that can't be traced back to a nation-state for retaliation."

"This being what your informant reported," the director said.

"Yes."

The room grew silent as we considered the potential consequences.

Someone once wrote that a meeting shouldn't be called unless the outcome is known. But here the innumerable presented facts gave no guidance, led to no path. The silence grew.

The Director looked expectantly toward us as he spoke, "The answers seem to lie in St. Louis."

"I planned to return," Kristin said.

"We admired your creativity there," the Director said.

Kristin smiled appreciatively. It was unlikely that such illegality had ever been praised in this building before.

Refreshments lay in an anteroom for the meeting's end. Though not hungry, I had anticipated the greater intimacy of this format and wasn't disappointed.

Chapter 88

Being a health-conscious eater, I filled my plate with pita, humus, and baked salmon. The Director moved to my side.

"Just the nutritious food that my wife presses on me," he said, looking down at my plate.

"It's what I tell my children. I would feel guilty doing otherwise," I said, expecting that personal sharing would benefit our collaboration.

"How many children do you have?" he asked.

"Four."

"You're young for that many responsibilities."

"Two are twins and one is a foster child," I said simply.

"With all your burden, it was kind to take on another responsibility."

"I felt I had no choice. She lived in my town and fled to my house after her parents were murdered. I'm an adoptee and it seemed natural."

We walked in silence to a sofa and it was a few moments before the Director spoke.

"Of course! You're *that* Margaret and she's Asya, the child who might someday be Queen of Russia."

"Possibly. Now she's our treasure and an adored big sister to the others," I said.

"And your father is a Russian general," he said.

"Retired and heading the security company where I work which has former CIA and British intelligence officials on its Board," I said.

Adding this information, which he likely knew, to underscore that I wasn't a foreign spy as some who know only patchy facts assume.

"What type of work does your husband do?"

"He's a computer scientist heading a start-up," I said.

"Our department could use his talent," the Director said.

"You almost had it. You offered him a scholarship when he was in high school but it came with strings. He's a complex guy."

"And you're a complex woman," he said, approvingly.

After munching on the salmon I abruptly asked, "Do you know about Prattle?"

Chapter 89

"I never heard of anything called Prattle," the Director said slowly.

"Trickery is good when battling enemies. Several years ago my husband's company was awarded a contract to develop a cyber-detection system that would reduce the capabilities of an attacker who had gained a foothold on a computer network," I said.

"It would do this by generating computer traffic to mislead the attacker, making them doubt what they learned or causing them to make mistakes that would increase their likelihood of being detected.

"Prattle observes local traffic to create traffic indistinguishable from it but slightly changed. This is used to direct the intruder toward fake workstations or servers, distracting them from real search terms or operational priorities.

"This false realistic traffic pushes the enemy to act in a way which makes them easier to detect or marks data so it can be tied to their location or time of activity. Or it might muddle the details of high value information, like source code or financial data, by inserting small variables into real documents to misdirect real interests."

"You believe that a foreign nation wants these crimes regarded as local police matters rather than as the lead-up to their main action so they could escape without retribution," the Director said.

"Would you take a small bet I'm right?" I asked, with a grin.

"Never from you! You stopped a bioterrorist attack on West Point," the Director said, emphatically.

"That was luck," I said.

"Napoleon said he always would always choose a lucky general over a smart one and I consider you both," he said.

I blushed, having never gotten over feeling embarrassed when being praised.

Chapter 90

Upon leaving the conference I asked Kristin, "When can you leave for St. Louis?"

"I'm packed. Be on a flight tomorrow," she said.

"Do you have a game plan?" I asked.

I had learned that while a manager should set goals they should leave how to carry them out to the employee.

"Not really. Just to chat-up Boots at the Sing Sing Bar and hope that something develops," Kristin said.

"It's a plan. If you need anything," I said approvingly, knowing there was nothing else she could do.

I had thought to add, "Good luck," but knew that the friendship that developed between us didn't need it. It would not wear out and need never be spoken of, containing a duty of sacrifice on call without mention.

Despite advances in technical intelligence using computers and camera-equipped satellites, the more difficult human-based spying is most valuable. Common sense and the ability to analyze character quickly and decisively are an intelligence agent's greatest assets and Kristin had these in spades. When she left, the room seemed to have become quiet. Like in those movies before you hear the screams of violence, I thought.

At home there were only normal sounds, of squabbling children and a hungry husband who had unexpectedly returned early.

Chapter 91

Despite Kristin's early (6AM) flight, I met her departure from Ronald Reagan Washington National Airport.

"Do you have all you need?" I asked.

Though this was unnecessary since she was more organized than any mother of young children can be.

"Two slut outfits. What more could I need?" she asked.

Her tone was humorous but she wasn't smiling.

"Don't take chances. I want you back healthy and in one piece!" I said emphatically.

The boarding call sounded. I touched her shoulder and she left.

A popular saying is that waiting is the hardest, whether for a marriage proposal, medical test result, or an ongoing operation. Even while being busy with family and business chores, thoughts about Kristin were never far from my mind. I found myself reaching for my phone though knowing that if help were needed, she or Otto would call.

Accompanying their silence were calls from the FBI seeking an update, of which there was none.

Only four days later did I receive a text from Kristin, "All well. I'm in." Learning this, my FBI contact asked, crudely, "Into Boots or their plan?" To which I shrugged, knowing that his comment just reflected the pressure which we all felt.

Stephanie's plight weighed on us, either as a child needing rescue or a body awaiting proper burial. Did Kristin question her mission or consider herself as a soldier, not to think but only to accomplish the job and get the hell out? I wondered.

It is a mistake to obsess about an operation's success since triumph requires mental disengagement. Your information sources aren't friends though you make them think they are. They are assets to be exploited until dry, then cast aside for fresher sources of data.

Soon, if a dozen things went right, I'd get another positive message from Kristin. And if another dozen things went right, Stephanie would return safely to her family.

Chapter 92

While fretting, I considered the impending disaster. To take down a nation's military brain an entire army and not just a handful of agents was needed. Coordinated surgical strikes against its leaders, perhaps one at a time, could be camouflaged as street crimes or accidents. Here, government alarm would be small, these events being interpreted as those of the crazed or street thugs. With the Department of Homeland Security in its usual bureaucratic muddle and the military forbidden by law from acting within America's boundaries, success would be probable.

But for such a crime to succeed its creator would need good recruits, with none having enough information to betray it or the others. Each murder must seem separate until the final cataclysmic blow. Which would be what? I fruitlessly asked myself.

I stopped theorizing, knowing that doing so without facts is worse than useless, leading one down a blind alley as Sherlock Holmes said. And, though he might have said but didn't, that given half a chance everyone becomes the hero of their own detective story.

Yet I *did* feel that events were moving toward their climax. Awful as were the prior crimes, none had gripped the nation's attention as did Stephanie's kidnapping. If the child of a major city's mayor was unsafe, what child is? Her friend, Louisa, who had been bound and stripped naked, stoked public alarm through her continuing interviews by empathetic reporters. Which she devotedly reported via the Facebook, Twitter, and Houseparty channels. Next she'll be marketing cosmetics, I thought snappishly.

"You look sad," my toddler daughter observed.

Being motherly proud of her observational skill, I replied honestly.

"I am sad. I'm worrying about a friend who is doing important work," I said.

"Sadness often has its own reward."

"Where did you hear that?" I asked, with surprise.

"In my religion class."

I should go to church more often, I thought, and hugged her.

Chapter 93

My reward might have been the thanks in an exuberant call from a friend, thanking me for my advice. The story is this.

Polly, who is also twenty-six, has a career far different from mine. A graduate of Harvard Law School, she worked at one of the multi-national law firms populating Manhattan.

Her leisure time consisted of having meals in pricey restaurants with equally high-earning female friends, none of whom had yet found a mate meeting their requirements: having a dynamite career, a great sense of humor, and yearning for marriage and children.

Despite extensive search, all of their prospects had lacked either income or elegance. One smoked, another forgot birthdays, others were too tied to their family and several (gasp!) actually preferred beer to wine. A cheesecake addiction might be tolerable but *that*?

Concern with safety had caused Polly to purchase a security system for her Manhattan condo. The installer arrived early on Saturday morning and was walked around the apartment by pajama-dressed Polly.

"He was a *hunk,*" she later told me, being in his late twenties, six-inches taller than her five-foot-ten, and built like a linebacker. His blue eyes and courteous manner aroused her thought of slipping from her pajamas into nothing.

After completing the installation, she offered him breakfast and things went from there. Oren had grown up in small-town Ohio. His father was a pharmacist and his mother a beautician. He was the oldest child, having four younger sisters that he'd often babysat.

Money was tight in the family so after graduating high school he joined the Marines where he received training in electronics. He had been sightseeing in Manhattan when he read a want-ad and that was it. He might want his own business someday but was in no hurry.

Polly's friends were horrified when she spoke about Oren since his shortcomings were obvious. He preferred beer to wine, permitted himself one cigar a day, and wore Walmart sport-clothes to gatherings. In short, he was *blue-collar.* But unlike some of the men that they'd known, he didn't tell dirty jokes or caress their butt, insulted no one, never raised his voice, and was unfailingly courteous.

"He can also fix things so I never have to worry and he's honest and reliable. I find myself wanting to do things for him, little things that I never did for another man. The sex is great and we have fun together."

Despite her friends' warnings, but with my continuing encouragement, Polly married Oren. "Things couldn't be better!" she gushed on the phone that morning.

Lifting my sadness was payment in full for my good deed.

Chapter 94

It wasn't only Kristin's peril that worried me but the government's reaction. Under unrelenting pressure, it degenerated into panic-stricken factions without leadership. The crisis needed not textbook orthodoxy but a rejection of dogma and artistic flexibility. Who would provide this? I wondered. This was understood by others but not their solution.

"They want *you,*" my father insisted during a quickly scheduled meeting.

"Me? I'm a stay-at-home mom," I said, incredulously.

"And a capable manager with a reputation for creativity that few can match. Your mother could care for the kids, which they would love as long as it takes," he said.

Of that I had no doubt since, unlike me, she considers sweets to be food. But refusing this request wasn't possible, not with my father's stance and employee's life on the line.

"However would I survive without you two," I said, accepting graciously.

Preparing my children presented no problem. Whatever qualms I had were dismissed by ten-year-old Asya. "Don't worry, we'll have lots of fun," she said. Promising to take care of everything, "except for the breastfeeding."

Though smiling, I felt uneasy at her undeniably funny remark, not wanting her to grow up so quickly. I would happily have my children prefer Disney comics until well into their adolescence, being shocked by the themes of suicide, alcoholism, and unwed pregnancy inhabiting young adult fiction.

With packed overnight bag in hand and reassuring comments ringing in my ears, I left the Watergate to enter the car awaiting me.

Chapter 95

The office that I was given wasn't large. Beint the size of a medium-sized bedroom it might have reflected how some bureaucrats regard women and where they prefer them. "A new manager's hardest battle is against deep-rooted bureaucracy," the father of my best friend, Erika, once said. Being a former math professor and current hedge fund owner he should know.

Moreover, the room's atmosphere indicated how matters stood. Because none work best when feeling hopeless, creating optimism and loyalty must begin with me, I told myself. I needed to be upbeat no matter the situation but this didn't mean ignoring what wasn't working.

Because eating reduces anxiety, I had arranged for beverages and snacks to be laid for my group. They were four men and two women, ranging in age from twenty-four to thirty-one and of varying background.

I had been given a file on each and was impressed. With such talent and intelligence we should be able to accomplish, I hoped, but was consumed by a personal thought when the first member arrived.

"I'm sorry to startle you, I should have knocked. I'm Tod Lanning," he said, apologetically.

"No, it's fine. I was puzzling over a friend's comment and being a man you might help," I said.

"Glad to if I can."

"It's about match-making," I said, hesitantly.

"If I can," Tod said, grinning.

"A single, thirty-year-old guy works at my husband's startup. He's had a string of bad relationships and dates and I wonder if what he said is true," I said.

"What's that?"

"That it's a mistake to date professional women. Not that wants a woman without opinions but he doesn't want to talk about economics or politics when he gets off work. The women that he's met seem to feel it compromises their self-worth to be feminine and sexy with a man. He likes doing things for them like opening a car door but when he does their reaction is often, 'I can do that for myself.' He said he's competitive at work but wants to leave it behind at home, not wanting to have to compete with his lover about income or when playing tennis or anything.

"It's not that he's interested in an unemployed dingbat since he does want a woman who works hard at whatever. But what's most important for him is that she's warm and honest and caring, just a nice person. Can he be right about professional women?" I asked.

"As right as rain. I have two graduate degrees, speak four languages besides English, and am happily married to a beautician. We care about each other and that's what's important, besides not being a dingbat of course."

The other committee members arrived just moments after Tod. While listening to our conversation, I saw them relax. Without intention I had accomplished my first goal.

Chapter 96

Now that my group was relaxed, I looked sternly about them, not wanting them to feel that they were dealing with Mrs. Mom.

"There are many books and movies involving terrorism: *The Sum of All Fears*, *The Peacemaker*, and the TV drama, *24*, in which terrorists are always a few ticks from achieving America's nuclear disaster. Americans have had so much entertainment on this issue that they feel adequately educated though few academics have thought through what happens in the months after an attack. This is partly because the government's response to such terrorism is unknowable.

"Anyone on the National Security Council will tell you that decisions of war and peace are partly the product of fickle factors like the president's personality and the people surrounding him. Because these and luck play a role in shaping White House discussions, realistic speculation is difficult. The wide range of possibilities and unknowable factors make it hard to prescribe policy.

"Another reason for this question not gaining an answer is that most consider it far less relevant than preventing the terrorism.

214

Thinking up responses to it is like considering the day after any disaster containing a unique scale of devastation.

"Does the national security apparatus focus on the government's potential response to an asteroid striking the planet or the aftermath of a war between China and the United States? It does not because these scenarios fall into the realm of the surreal or, at a minimum, a situation when there is such massive social disruption and severe decrease of government capacity that it is difficult to even know where to begin. Only an unusually brave politician would publicly focus on the day after instead of the days before. Accepting such terrorism is an unacceptable position which his opponents would contemptuously reject.

"And if an attack did occur, who would the nation's military retaliate against if its origin is unclear. Would a nuclear retaliation causing the death of millions who had nothing to do with it be accepted?

"The great Prussian military theorist, Carl von Clausewitz, observed that the fog of war is a permanent condition of armed conflict. But it is also true that the density of this fog shifts over time, growing and scattering with the increase in intelligence."

My spiel gained their attention. All had stopped eating and stared as Carol asked, "What intelligence do we have?"

Chapter 97

Many bureaucrats gain promotion by passing blame or, in the words of a famed World War Two general whose name escapes me, "having a talent for kissing ass."

So before answering Carol's question, which was likely held by the others, I asked myself, How can I get them to take seriously what I say? Then, as can happen, a thought struck me.

Asya, my ten-year-old ward, had a life filled with change both bad and good. Endangered since birth, her identify had been hidden from her by her adoptive parents. When considering her background, it is understandable why truth became a crucial matter for her. She had made me promise two things: that I would never abandon her, which was easy to do; and that she would ask me one question each week and receive a truthful answer no matter the question.

I hesitated as you might expect. When Asya entered adolescence, would she probe my sex life? But I agreed, knowing that she was sensible beyond her years and haven't regretted it. Most of her interest lay in my work.

Thus what I said to these junior bureaucrats was something they would likely never hear on any job. "Though new to government work, I already understand that a cardinal principal is to avoid responsibility for a failure lest it impinge on your career. It won't be this way here. I will take all responsibility for failure and answer every question honestly. Each of you may now ask one question. I'll consider Carol's first."

Chapter 98

"There aren't as many facts to rumor as I would like. Our agent learned the name of a man who was approached to do something having a huge effect but not exactly what it is," I said.

"What has he learned?" Jud asked.

"Only that a religious proclamation would be issued stating that God would strike the unbelievers blind on a particular day and it would actually happen," I said.

"That isn't possible," Jud insisted.

"Yes, it would be though not easy to carry out. There is a flower which, when combined with a volatile liquid, produces mustard gas, a widely used World War I chemical agent. In an enclosed space it fries the cornea. But intelligence would be needed about when and where the targets would be together, and how to place the device in the room," Lisa said.

"We don't know who the confederates are or if they're in the government," I said.

"Then anything could be possible," Jud said.

I simply nodded, there being nothing to say.

"How long has your agent been in place?" Joseph asked.

"A few days. She's contacted our target and is getting close so we can only wait and hope," I said.

"What are her Rules of Engagement?" Joseph asked.

"She has none," I said.

"None?" he asked, with surprise.

"Just the motto of my company: there is a justice of lawyers and the courtroom, and a justice of The Prophets and of God. And if she doesn't succeed, God help America," I said.

I felt like adding, *and particularly us*, but didn't.

Chapter 99

That there were no further questions satisfied me since my intent had been to create a trusting mood rather than provide information. Looking about the room, I summarized the situation.

"There's general agreement that the spate of shocking crimes are a smokescreen by a terrorist group to conceal their intention to decapitate America's military. How this is intended we don't yet know but my agent will hopefully provide this shortly.

"You should expect to be on-call 24/7. Whether the action comes this week or next I can't say but my instinct tells me that it won't be much beyond then. Stephanie's kidnapping shocked the world so their next move should be *it*."

"So we just sit and wait till then?" Carol asked.

Though sensing this to be more a political ploy than serious question, I responded calmly.

"No. You're going to research the many ways that America's military can be decapitated and even what this means. Is it murdering personnel or taking control of computer systems and how can their security be strengthened? It's a big job and you'll be busy. I'll be in touch."

"How did it go?" the Director asked.

"Well, for a start. I seemed to have gained enough of their trust so they'll be more concerned with accomplishment than politics," I said.

"That's a persisting danger of all bureaucracies," he said.

"It brought about the 9/11 terror attack disaster," I said.

The Director didn't reply. The battling of FBI and CIA personnel, because of which critical information that might have prevented the attack hadn't been shared, was widely condemned in the aftermath. No one wanted a repeat.

Chapter 100

Filled with fear, I waited like everyone else, for more information and theories but hopefully no more terrible events. Continuing fear raises tension and arouses anxieties unrelated to the real danger. A normal medical symptom is viewed as catastrophic, and a dress returned stained from the cleaners causes uncommon protest. My upset concerned my upcoming birthday. Not a worry about surviving until then but because of my husband's probable gift.

Before hearing my criticism you should know that Randy is a wonderful husband. He's supportive of my difficult work schedule and is a great father, having even diapered our babies and how many fathers do you know do that? But, and possibly because he was an only child, his one glaring marital fault is that he doesn't react to my birthday as I think he should.

In my family of four girls, birthdays were a big event with our present being a combination of Christmas and the Fourth of July in one beribboned package. But for Randy, whose father is an unemotional surgeon and his mother is a busy civic club president, a birthday was just another day. His parents do love him but emotions aren't their style.

So, being married to a sign-it-quick, Hallmark kind of guy whose (practical) birthday present is something like a faster laptop (Randy is a computer geek), I suffer in silence though having explained how important my birthday is to me.

So I approach each of my birthdays with anxiety, knowing that despite Randy's high intelligence he simply can't get it emotionally. I would someday adjust to his quirk but hadn't yet. My phone's chime thrust me from my personal funk back into the world.

Chapter 101

This phone call wasn't the crisis that I feared but the pleasant resolution of a recent case.

Josef, one of our bodyguard employees, had been made a puzzling job offer by Clinton, a local corporate CEO: to murder him in exchange for a two-hundred-thousand-dollar payment. Explaining this weird request by stating that he was dying of cancer and wanted his wife to collect on an insurance policy through an apparent burglary-murder. Our investigation found that both his company and marriage were on the rocks and that's where matters had stood.

"Have you discovered anymore?" I asked Josef.

"I have the two-hundred-thousand and it's over," he said, smugly.

"What happened?" I asked.

"You won't believe it or why he chose me."

Josef is another of those exasperating people who string out stories.

"Tell me," I said patiently.

"We managed to hack into his doctor's records. He's perfectly healthy unlike his business and marriage. Do you remember my telling you of our bodily likeness?"

"Yes," I said slowly.

"Well, his plan was to murder me during payment and substitute my body for his, destroying identifying features in a fire. The authorities would have *his* body, their case would be closed, and he'd be off with his girlfriend and money embezzled from his company. It would have worked if my gun hadn't been quicker."

"He's dead?" I asked.

"It couldn't be avoided. He'd boasted of his plan while holding a gun on me but wasn't familiar with it. I bashed his head with a fireplace anvil before he could get the safety off. Then took the money, cleaned off fingerprints, put him in his car with whiskey poured over him, and drove it off a cliff. A fire broke out and the police will consider it a simple DWI."

"That problem is solved. Do you plan to retire with the money?" I asked.

"Two-hundred-thousand isn't much today. Besides, people like me shouldn't retire. Working keeps them sane.," Josef said.

"That it can do," I agreed.

Chapter 102

It is a mistake to think that anything can happen despite being fairly sure what will. If hopelessness was a color, the room's mood would have been shades of black.

"We have new information," I said.

Using the pronoun "we" to foster group cohesiveness. Their mood seemed to lighten as they stared expectantly.

"A foreign sleeper agent has lived in America since their teenage years, becoming steeped in our culture and burrowing deep within our social fabric. They have access to the highest levels of government but we have not yet learned their identity," I said.

"This information came from your agent?" Carol asked.

"Yes."

"And what do we do now?" she asked.

Her tactic was obvious. If I said "nothing" and disaster ensued, she might wriggle from blame. Obviously, my attempt to foster group unity hadn't been completely successful. Then again, optimism seemed to come with my blood and isn't a universal trait, I reminded myself.

"We think up scenarios in which America's military could be eliminated in one fell swoop and defenses against them. After foiling this one, there will certainly be others and though one shouldn't depend on being lucky, diligence—hard work—is its mother."

Two days later, I read their memos of potential threats. Though impressed with the speed of their responses, their ideas were uninspiring, the stuff of generations of novels. The poisoning of the Pentagon's or a military bases' water supply. Sabotaging the guidance system of a nuclear missile so it struck the nation's capital. Assassinating the President. But how could a lone sleeper agent cause any of these? I asked myself.

Chapter 103

Leaving the office feeling depressed disappointed, I did what I had neglected doing and still hesitate revealing: seeking help from the spirit world.

I have earlier written how I adopted the African religion of Santeria after being healed of what was considered an incurable genetic disorder. This was achieved by my parents following the advice of a Greenwich teacher, Mother Marie, who had been tutoring my sister in French. A Santeria priestess, she prayed and then dreamed that my cure lay in eating soybeans which is now the standard treatment for Sanfilippo Disease.

Despite Mother Marie's miracle, I didn't abandon my family's Mormon heritage. "The Gods are not jealous," she told me.

I may be wrong to relate my improved mood to spiritualism. Taking a hot bath is common though mine involved cleansing with Sunflower and Patchouli soap from a botanica's online store. I wouldn't presume to have received spiritual aid though feel a spiritual force afterward. Or, if spiritual is the wrong word, something akin to the power that a lion feels in the presence of its tamer. An assurance that I felt I could communicate to my group, though hoping not to sound like Joan of Arc.

My study group was the smallest of the units involved. It was intended as an idea factory, a mini think tank of the brightest. Despite this their ideas had been pedestrian, just marginally better than a college student would produce.

The crucial answer came from an unlikely source, one of those conversations about nothing that become fixed in memory.

Chapter 104

Inescapable biology having reared its head, my youngest teenage sister, Claudine, asked her question while eating an ice cream cone.

"How much of dating is real and how much is fairy tale like a Hollywood movie?"

"You'd better sit down. This'll take a while," I said, taking more time than needed to refill my apple juice while collecting my thoughts.

"You're right. There is real dating and movie dating with the two rarely intersecting. Children grow up on fairy tales and adults substitute their own. There's the fairy tale which believes that when a man says he'll call he actually will. There's the fairy tale of a man still in love with a past love and only half present when he's with you no matter what he says. There's the fairy tale of believing that all men speak honestly and don't play games until you realize that everyone plays games but not always by the same rules.

"There's the fairy tale of the man who seems perfect for you, he offering a great package until you realize that it's empty. There's also the fairy tale that dating is fun which is held by women who dream about how the first date will be down to what they'll eat. It's a sweet daydream but is usually abandoned during one's twenties," I said.

Claudine had stopped licking her melting ice cream, appearing crushed by the weight of my facts.

"This isn't what you expected," I observed.

"Hardly. What's the worst dating fairy tale of all?" she asked.

"When a man says he's leaving his wife because she refuses to have sex," I said.

"How would you know?" Claudine asked.

"One certainty is when she becomes pregnant," I said.

We sat silently in the comfortable silence we always enjoy. Her next statement startled me.

"I just finished a novel that predicted the crimes that've been happening. Maybe it's like Sherlock Holmes said, 'It's a wicked world and when a brilliant man turns to crime it's the worst of all.'"

Chapter 105

Years before, I and my best friend, Erika, had a dinnertime lesson from her very smart father. It went something like this.

"People make decisions based on *occasion noise* or *deliberation*. Occasion noise is the attention that is driven by random variations in whatever grabs your notice at the moment. So reading about a disaster might cause you to be wary of investing in a risky investment and being angry might cause you to buy more of one of your falling assets. The opposite of this *noise* isn't *quiet* but doing things in a disciplined, reasoned way, organizing your thinking so it is as intentional as possible."

Erika interrupted her father's monologue to ask, "How do you do that?"

He smiled broadly before answering, being pleased that she was listening closely. As was I, following my habit of paying close attention to the words of every expert.

"To begin, you must keep in mind that first impressions are dangerous since you'll interpret later information in ways consistent with whatever you learned first which will bias your final decision. To avoid this, use a checklist to structure your questions and the evidence you seek to answer them.

"Break your decision into its components. As an example, if you're considering buying into a company, evaluate their capacity to innovate, their customer loyalty, their financial strength, and the quality of their management, on a scale of one to ten to keep one good quality from casting a halo over the others.

"Then get second opinions, asking different people the same questions or even yourself the same questions at different times to reduce *noise* and wait as long as you can before deciding. In a world filled with noise, being disciplined is your greatest strength."

Thus though Claudine's information had struck a nerve, I remembered Erika's father's advice and didn't act immediately. Instead after reading the novel, I planned to re-read it before asking myself the critical questions: How closely do real events mirror those in the book, and who is its author?

Chapter 106

A popular myth, that things get easier as you get older, might only be true of those who aren't mothers. While I had planned to immediately re-read the book that Claudine spoke of, *Armageddon America*, a family duty intervened: reading newly purchased books to my toddlers who insisted that I read them *now* and the safety of the republic be damned. So I did.

Of course both were picture books. The first, *Is Was*, begins with massing rainclouds followed by a chain of events: a chipmunk and bird sipping from puddles of rainwater, then fleeing after being surprised by a fox as a bee flies past. We follow the bee as it travels past sunflowers, to be joined by other wild creatures and finally a human family.

The second book, *How to Apologize*, teaches this in a humorous, age-appropriate tone when an alligator is surprised in his bath by a parachuting penguin crashing through the roof. Animals model kindness and sorrow, as when a porcupine apologizes for popping a squirrel's balloon.

I had hoped to return to *my* book after reading these but it was not to be. They insisted, without apology, that we read another of their books and took turns reading aloud.

This picture book, their favorite, is the most recent in a series about a bad-tempered bear. Here, he is so fed-up with everyone's clamoring for fun that he goes fishing by himself. Unfortunately, the bear's fun-loving twin turns up with rowdy friends and a day-long, candy-eating fest ensues. After the house is trashed, the bear returns to restore order.

Hmm...like when I return home after the children's grandparents babysit them, I thought.

Chapter 107

The novel, *Armageddon America*, by Elliot Buford Wellday, had been published two years before and wasn't a big seller. It received no Amazon reviews or Google mention but the same could not be said for its author.

Wellday had an impressive military background, having attended the Army War College and written numerous professional articles on wide ranging topics that included the limits of deterrence of nuclear weapons, the tendency of soldiers to avoid primary health care, and the legislative agendas of veterans serving in state legislatures.

He was forty-seven, had served in the Special Forces, been a military attaché, and trained foreign soldiers in the Middle East and Africa. Holding the rank of Colonel, he served on the National Security Council, America's principal forum for considering national security and foreign policy matters, helping the president to coordinate these among government agencies.

Re-reading the book evidenced why it hadn't sold. The writing was wooden, the ending was depressing (which readers don't like), and the protagonist was unpleasant, believing that women prefer dominating men and experiencing pain during intimacy. In one coupling, he entered here anally while biting her earlobe and gripping her pubic hair. But, as Claudine said, the crimes that it contained *did* mirror what happened in America. Even down to the kidnapping of the mayor's daughter though in the book it was a governor's daughter that was abducted. Was Wellday was psychic or...?

I ordered copies of *Armageddon America* and called a meeting of my FBI group for the following day. The book wouldn't arrive by then but there were other things to do. I wanted a psychological profile of Wellday *now*.

Chapter 108

The group pushed back against my idea. Either because it seemed bizarre that a criminal would advertise their crimes or from habit. Would they react similarly to a male boss? I wondered, before dismissing this thought as irrelevant and assigning tasks.

A psychological profile requires background and current information. Who were Wellday's parents? Does he have siblings? Who were his high school friends and what were his teachers' opinions? Did he ever use drugs or alcohol and to what degree? What is his life like apart from the military?

I wanted to know *everything*, including how upset he got when shopping in the military commissary, which is a retail store selling name-brand products tax-free at lower prices than regular stores. Military families usually shop on weekends with Sundays being particularly busy. How does Wellday react when stuck in a line with child-laden families pushing *two* grocery carts? This would try anyone's patience.

"Why is that important?" Carol had asked.

"Because when creating a psychological profile you don't know what information is important and so must collect everything. You can always have too little but never too much data," I rejoined.

To maintain confidentiality, I relied on my company to provide it. Wellday might just be an unusually creative and innocent military officer. To involve him in a government investigation would tarnish his reputation and ruin his chance for promotion. It wouldn't be fair.

My workers got busy. As Wellday's life came into focus, one fact stood out: that while all considered him smart, resourceful, and conscientious, none considered him more than a mere acquaintance no matter how long they had worked together. For a military officer to be friendless is odd since comradeship is a career benefit. Nor did he have a wife.

Chapter 109

Since becoming a manager, I often reminded myself of an old adage: that the obedience of employees can be demanded but their loyalty must be won. As the facts about Wellday trickled in, the group's cohesion increased as they changed from paperwork pushing, politically striving bureaucrats into hunters.

We pored over the interviews with his teachers. Many remembered him for having achieved an outstanding career despite his dismal background.

Wellday's father was an occasional auto mechanic and committed drunk. His mother was a beaten-down figure prone to frequent bruises that were self-described as "accidents." She worked as an R.N. in a doctor's office and managed a day care center that she owned. Her hard work had granted the family a middle-class lifestyle.

Neither of Wellday's two older sisters had turned out well, they becoming unwed, drug-addicted mothers. The oldest also had serious mental problems and both lost custody of their children to the grandparents. Unsurprisingly, Wellday didn't visit his family nor did they attend his graduations. He explained this by lying that his entire family had been wiped out in an auto accident.

At West Point. Wellday had been marked by his classmates as "a comer" but odd. Not with visible weirdness but by not being one of them. The women that he dated had sensed this too. One said, "He went through the normal motions but it was as if he weren't there. Or if he was, that he was studying you without passion, like you were a fetal pig on a dissecting table." This might be why his longest intimate relationship seems to have been two months.

Chapter 110

Besides Wellday's emotional detachment, what all of his girlfriends mentioned was his cruelty: that lovemaking for him seemed to require their pain. Most hadn't objected to his preference for anal sex with several stating that it had aroused their powerful orgasm. What had disturbed them was that during the sex, he had tightly held their pubic hair and bit their earlobe. "Using my ass was OK but not pain," one woman said, without the trace of embarrassment. Another of his favored practices was binding a woman's hands to the bedframe. All had objected to this though one said, "It was my freaky time."

Carol dramatically dropped her sheaf of papers.

"Has anyone noticed the string of torture killings in Seoul when Wellday was stationed there?" she asked.

We pored over the translated news articles and those that had hit the English language wire services. While all were blood-curdling, one crime was distinct since this victim wasn't a prostitute like the others and another motive was present.

Margaret in Washington

This sixteen-year-old girl had prominent parents, her (single) mother being an actress and her (deceased) father having been a noted author. The kidnapper's ransom demand followed the mother's receipt of a photo of her daughter's nude body and pieces of her fingers. Delivering the payment proved difficult with several drop-offs being aborted because the kidnapper saw police and TV reporters trailing. The media hadn't respected the news blackout and had camped outside the mother's home.

All attempts to pay the ransom failed and, following the last, a letter in English was mailed to the mother stating where her daughter could be found. She was, having been dead for three days after being raped and forced to ingest urine, feces, and laundry detergent.

Stunned silence filled the room after Carol's presentation. "Let's take a fifteen-minute break," I said.

Chapter 111

The horrific killings still consumed minds when we reconvened.

"I can understand a soldier killing honorably since it's in defense of their country. But to act on a civilian..." Carol said.

Though this topic detracted from the central issue, there had seemed no way to avoid it. And relating to it might pull them from their ivy-tower mentality, I thought.

"Carol is correct," I said supportively. "To kill deliberately is emotionally crushing except for those who are seriously disturbed even if they appear okay. But such actions are sometimes needed for the greater good and would find favor in the eyes of Heaven too," I said.

"I can't see that. Give an example," asserted Andrew, a Yale Law School graduate.

I hesitated before answering, being concerned with the risk of gossip.

"I'll speak hypothetically," I began. "A politician of a major nation plans a coup to convert it into a dictatorship similar to those of Hitler and Stalin and Mao. This would cause many civilian deaths, much public hardship, and nuclear peril for the world.

"Learning this, an agent thwarts his agenda by killing him without formal government approval. Did the agent do right? Would you back their prosecution or applaud them for potentially saving millions of lives? Tell me," I said.

My tone hadn't apparently been as cool as I hoped since several gave me the look of children who sense they had been told a lie.

"You're telling a true story," Peter asserted.

"Stick to the issue," I retorted.

But he was right.

Chapter 112

I had been sent to Moscow to investigate the rumor that a retired assassin became active. Being chosen because we had once lived together and she considered me her friend.

The events that followed, though never revealed publicly, existed in rumor. That an American politician was to be murdered as pretext for a coup in Russia, to install a Stalin-type dictatorship with the coup leader at its head. A plot that might have succeeded had he not been assassinated by an unknown American woman who left Russia before its borders were sealed and was never heard of again.

Which I knew to be true since I was that woman. The rumor was ignored by both nations, it having been decided that confirming it would harm the peaceful sleep of many. I answered Peter's assertion with an event that I could reveal. Part of it, that is.

"It's not easy to kill someone. For soldiers it's a matter of kill or be killed and to protect their country. Moreover, these killings are usually done at a distance with the targets being vague. There have been studies of soldiers who kill high-value terrorists using remotely controlled drones from thousands of miles away. You would think this wouldn't disturb these soldiers since it would seem like playing a video game but you'd be wrong.

"It's hard to kill someone that you've watched via satellite video-feed over a period of time. You try to hit them when they're alone so the strike won't harm others. You see them playing outside with their children and shopping with their wife and start to feel almost their friend. To kill them you must remind yourself of the murders and bombings this terrorist engaged in. But even with a clear conscience, killing arouses an emotional cost regardless of the distance and how much the target deserves to die."

Chapter 113

My indirect answer was enough to quell the group's interest in my life. Fantasizing about one's boss is universal and particularly since I had been forced upon their careers. Does this expensively dressed woman bearing a Mamma Shark tote know *anything*? Or is she a hack who was forced on the FBI for the sake of political correctness. With the air cleared and having recovered from the torture-murder description, we returned to business.

"What more do we know about Wellday?" I asked.

"One oddity is that he's completely out of touch when on vacation. He's supposed to leave a number and does but on the few times that it's been called, for nothing more serious that a paperwork deadline, he didn't return the call. The numbers keep changing as if they were burner phones he discards," Carol said.

"So we don't know where he goes," I mused.

"He could be off killing anywhere," Paul said.

All seemed to have accepted, as fanciful as it initially seemed, that Wellday's book,

Armageddon America, contained the blueprint of an impending catastrophe by a warped personality who must be stopped.

I welcomed the next question, having almost forgotten that matter as we concentrated on Wellday.

"Do we know more about the kidnapped mayor's daughter?"

"Yes. My agent thinks she might be held in an abandoned warehouse on the East St. Louis waterfront. She's trying to learn more and will call me tonight," I said.

I glanced deliberately at the wall clock and ended the meeting. The room cleared, I began gathering my papers, and Peter approached.

"It would look bad if an officer of Wellday's rank were branded a traitor," he said.

"Yes, it would," I agreed.

I stopped what I was doing and he waited for more.

"But I have an idea how to avoid it," I said briefly.

Chapter 114

I was reading in my tiny office when Bradley popped in. Being the only member of my group with a doctorate, he had casually mentioned this at our first meeting. He was a little over six-foot tall with a slender face, pale blue eyes, and a complexion that women would envy. His clothes were expensive and I remembered that his family was monied. He looked troubled.

It might have been my being a mother that invited his confidence. But considering his problem, it was more likely my working at a personal security company. I invited him to sit down and he carefully closed the door. I noticed the bruise on his face when he turned.

"You've been injured," I said.

"A mugging," he explained tersely.

I waited, sensing that more was coming.

"I need help with a personal problem."

"That's my day job," I said.

"The Director must not learn of it," he said.

"He won't from me unless it involves a crime or concerns our work," I said.

"I have a fiancée and behaved stupidly," he said.

"Relationships can be awkward and people make mistakes," I said supportively.

"It started during the big rainstorm two weeks ago. It was hard getting a taxi and as soon as I got into one, a woman asked if I minded sharing. We were going in the same direction and chatted. When it came to pay, I found that I had forgotten my wallet and had no money. She smiled, offered to pay my share, and said that I could make it up to her next time. She was expensively dressed and the charge was only fifteen dollars so I just thanked her with a smile and left. A week later we shared a taxi again."

Chapter 115

Distrusting coincidence, I felt a chill. Bradley paused and I asked, "What happened then?"

"What shouldn't have, I invited her for a drink and we talked. She said that she was stuck in a lousy marriage to a rich real-estate guy. The only good to come from it was her three-year-old daughter who she doted on. Leaving him wasn't possible since he'd hire the best divorce lawyer, make up lies to gain the child's custody and maybe kidnap her to Greece. He has dual citizenship and she'd never see her again.

"She was so tragic and lovely that it seemed natural to accept her suggestion that we stop at a hotel we just passed. While embraced in our room, a man holding a pistol burst in."

Bradley paused again but now I waited, not wanting to interrupt the flow.

"'You should have chained the door,' the intruder said, with a smile. I went at him but he easily swatted me away and kicked me in the stomach. While I gasped on the ground, naked and feeling helpless, he ripped off Dee's clothes and raped her. Then he grabbed our wallets, taking the money and driver licenses. 'You're not married. I wonder what your spouses would say about you two being here. Maybe I'll tell them,' he said, throwing me atop Dee and taking pictures before leaving. After gaining my breath, I said, 'We have to call the police.'"

"We can't, my husband would divorce me. Let's just get out of here and forget it," she insisted.

"That's what we did," Bradley said.

Chapter 116

Bradley had looked close to tears. In most thrillers, deeply distraught characters are given whiskey. Being a non-drinking Mormon, I supplied a grape juice from the mother's carryall that accompanies me.

"Drink it," I ordered, and he did.

Food relieves anxiety and it worked with him.

"Tell me what's really troubling you," I suggested softly.

Bradley swallowed before answering.

"Dee phoned me two days later. The robber called, wanting ten-thousand dollars not to send the pictures to her husband and she doesn't have it. He keeps her on a tight budget. She asked my help and I felt I had no choice, that it was the honorable thing to do. He just called her again. Now he wants another thirty-thousand dollars."

"Blackmailers don't give up on a good mark," I said calmly.

Bradley was a rising star in the FBI and came from a wealthy family. His father's law firm worked for both political parties. Though liking Bradley, my offer to help him was all business.

"Do you want my help in ending this problem?" I asked.

"Yes," he said calmly, having regained self-control.

"Okay, then do exactly as I say. Tell Dee it'll take time to get the money. In three days, the time that it'll take for me to make my arrangements, give her the money but only in a public place. Say that you fear being mugged carrying around so much cash. When she shows up, give her the money, return to your fiancée, and stray no more," I said.

"That's it?" Bradley asked.

"That's it."

"What will you do?"

"End your problem. You've been the target of an old con. I'll give odds that Dee is the girlfriend of her alleged rapist with the rest of her story being lies, that there's no husband or child," I said.

I stood to indicate that our meeting was over.

"I'll be forever grateful to you," he said, giving me a firm handshake.

Margaret in Washington

That's my intention, I thought.

Chapter 117

When selecting an agent to help Bradley, I decided to solve two problems simultaneously and hired David. A former Mossad agent, he had married an American girl and lived in Annapolis which is a short drive from Washington. High-level personal security is a narrow business world and rumor had it that he was available I phoned him, shared the benefits of working for our company, and we met for discussion at my apartment.

"I've heard of your company," David said.

"Only good things, I hope."

"*Definitely* good."

"We have a situation that need be dealt with. Are you available for a short-term job? If it works out I'll offer a permanent one," I said.

"A test?" he asked rhetorically, with a smile.

"You can call it that. You'll be paid twenty-five-thousand dollars for a job that may take only a few days and likely not more than two weeks. If you succeed, we'll throw in first-class airfare and five-thousand dollars spending money to wherever you and your wife would like to vacation," I said.

As I expected, David was speechless. Contrary to popular belief, governments don't pay intelligence agents highly.

"Your company is generous," he said.

"Because we demand a lot."

"Tell me the job," he said.

I did and asked, "How would you deal with it?"

"I've handled similar. Your mark probably isn't the couple's first con, they doing it regularly. After Bradley meets the woman, I'll follow her and intervene in their next act. Then make sure that they never do it again."

"There is a justice of lawyers and the courtroom, and a justice of The Prophets and of God," I said.

"I couldn't agree more," he said.

This being my company's motto, I felt sure that David would be a great hire.

Chapter 118

During the days before I heard from David, Bradley contributed only fitfully to the group. One day his distress was so apparent that I signaled for him to remain when the others left.

"You'll have to relax. The others have noticed," I said.

"I can't get that scene out of my mind. When he hit me with the pistol my shock turned from fear to absolute terror. I've never been hit before. I can't sleep. I feel like I'm in a middle of a nightmare. My fiancée has noticed too," he said.

"Try! Get busy helping her plan the wedding," I said.

"There won't be one if she learns about Dee."

"Trust me. It'll soon be over."

I tried to sound reassuring despite knowing that fate can throw curves and life holds no guarantees.

Meanwhile, I had been marked as sympathetic by another man. Philip, my husband's friend, phoned to commiserate. At twenty-six he was already a rising star in the computer industry.

"I'm considered *nice, the* kind, supportive guy who'll always cheer your bad day. I've been in love twice. The first time lasted four months with all seeming rosy until she looked like I'd given her dog droppings for a present. She told me we were over, that she'd been dating me on the rebound from her past boyfriend and they got back together. What made it worse is that he's a total loser with a prison record.

"My next love informed me that she was pregnant during our second month together, that the baby's father was her last boyfriend and they were getting married. He's twenty-four, a high school dropout and unemployed. I've come to believe that good guys finish last with most women."

Now you have another job I told myself: to find Philip a wife.

Chapter 119

Because Bradley's mood was upsetting our group, I was relieved when David contacted me.

"It's all over and time for my vacation," he said, with a big smile.

"How did you do it?" I asked, smiling.

"It wasn't hard though one should never tell this to their boss. I followed Dee until she took the next mark to a hotel room. When her boyfriend burst in to do his act, I corralled them at gunpoint and sent the mark on his way. Once he was gone, the boyfriend grabbed for his gun, missing me but shooting Dee. I killed him, put my gun in Dee's hand and fired a shot to leave powder residue. I left before the police arrived at an apparent double murder scene."

"I *am* impressed. Would you like to work for us?" I asked.

"Is your salary as generous as my fee for this job?" David asked.

"We try. You'll start at two-hundred-thousand-dollars a year plus company car. We offer a housing allowance like in the military, four weeks vacation the first year and six weeks thereafter, a fully paid health plan, and a retirement plan better than most. Before coming on you must meet our CEO in Berlin but I don't expect a problem. You can take your wife on another vacation."

"Your CEO is a Russian general, isn't he?" David asked.

"He's long retired from that service. Our Board consists of retired CIA and British intelligence officials and we work only for Western countries. You won't find an ethical issue," I said.

"It's a deal," David said, extending his hand.

Chapter 120

There is a progression to most cases. Some, as Bradley's, are resolved quickly but others take longer, as if unknowable fate must play its role to trouble humanity.

My group was wearing down. We had read the reports on Wellday's life, his military career and romantic attachments, and pored over his novel. Instinct told me he was the one we sought, the backstage actor behind the criminal madness that enveloped America. He didn't carry out these acts but his was intended as the climactic scene, the crushing of America's military might as in *Armageddon America*.

Confirmation arrived through my gifted husband's computer search which found a cabin that Wellday owned under the corporate name of Happy Days, Inc.

An illegal but morally defensible break-in, conducted while Wellday was in Washington, revealed a trove of information: large payments from a bank linked to the Iranian Revolutionary Guard, incriminating phone recordings he had made for some incomprehensible reason, and his plan. Which was so simple that I cursed myself for not thinking of it.

The President and many military officials would be present at the opening of a state-of-the-art, underground intelligence facility intended to be impervious to missile or biological attack. Nothing short of a direct nuclear blast could harm its inhabitants but Wellday had planned something ingenious.

Pieces of its custom designed furniture had been packed with explosives to be detonated remotely by a phone signal. This would be sent to the cellphone that was always carried by Wellday's superior who would be present at the event. The explosion would collapse the structure, killing all within. The furniture had been delivered by Happy Days, Inc.

Undoubtedly, Wellday would pass on this gala to relax at his well-stocked retreat, perhaps contemplating a sequel to *Armageddon America.*

Chapter 121

My adoptive father was a widely respected lawyer and judge before becoming a United States senator and I cherish his advice.

He had asked me to meet a friend, a partner in a law firm that had handled sensitive political matters since the Roosevelt administration. No reason was given but I was told it was important, that friends like him were worth having.

From our encounter came my need to make a risky decision, whether to aid the nation by committing an illegal but morally justified act. Was it better to prosecute an officer, placing an enduring shame on the military, or to provide the nation with an uplifting story following its string of tragedies. "It's your call," my dad said.

The government's dilemma was not *whether* to stop Wellday but how to do it without staining the nation's honor. The correct choice was obvious. "It would be best for the country were Wellday not arrested. We need a favor, Margaret," the lawyer had said.

"There is a justice of lawyers and the courtroom, and a justice of The Prophets and of God," I told him after presenting my solution. He nodded, smiled, and offered me his hand before leaving. "If you ever need a favor, *any* favor..." he said.

We had no written agreement but something stronger, and my choice wasn't just civic but business. "By protecting important people you gain immense power since they know it is you who is doing it," my father had told me.

The successful rescue of the mayor's daughter made the biggest headlines. The death of a military officer by a propane gas explosion at his summer cabin was only a brief story in some newspapers, the tragic end to a promising officer.

Nothing was said about his background or the novel he wrote. Nor was an autopsy conducted, one that would have found the bullet in his head. Accomplishing this was David's last task before his vacation.

And that was that.

Chapter 122

"You're worn out," Randy observed.

"I am," I admitted.

One benefit of a good marriage is having what might be considered a live-in therapist, a person who knows you as well as and occasionally better than you know yourself.

"It's been a rough time. After the pandemic came the crime wave. Then our move to Washington and all that's gone on here," I said.

"Which you handled extraordinarily well judging by Vladimir's praise," Randy said.

Surprisingly, he and Vladimir had become close, having weekly telephone conversations despite their vastly different backgrounds, one being a retired Russian general and the other a scholarly computer nerd.

"He's checking up on me," I said, with amusement.

"He always does but with affection. You're his daughter and will be the company's next CEO someday," Randy said.

"I hope he's hedging his bets," I said.

"You don't want to be the big cheese?"

"Only in our family," I said playfully, unbuttoning his pajamas.

Later, as we lay relaxed, I asked, "How did Philip's date work out?"

With Wellday's demise, the crime wave's end, and Kristin and David's reassignments, my routine business tasks were being done by my assistant in Greenwich. So I had the time to find a wife for Randy's friend, Philip.

The week earlier he met my latest candidate: the stunning daughter of a neighbor. After my two previous matches that were pleasant but didn't ring his bells, I was anxious to hear how my latest had turned out.

"You're a talented cupid," Randy said cryptically.

"*Well*?" I asked, expectantly.

"*Well*...they kissed at the end of their date."

"*And*?"

"Phillip said that he let himself go during the kiss and now, for the first time, he knows what real love is."

"Maybe I should be a matchmaker," I said, snuggling closer.

"So what's your next venture?" Randy asked, in a whisper.

I simply smiled.

www.ingramcontent.com/pod-product-compliance
Lightning Source LLC
Chambersburg PA
CBHW070853250626
47159CB00003B/1053